A FOREST WORLD

Also by Felix Salten

Bambi
Renni the Rescuer

A FOREST WORLD

FELIX SALTEN

Translation by PAUL R. MILTON
and SANFORD JEROME GREENBURGER

Aladdin
New York   London   Toronto   Sydney   New Delhi

ALADDIN

An imprint of Simon & Schuster Children's Publishing Division
1230 Avenue of the Americas, New York, NY 10020
This Aladdin hardcover edition October 2013
Text copyright © 1942 by The Bobbs-Merrill Company, copyright renewed
© 1970 by Anna Katharina Wyler-Salten and Simon & Schuster, Inc.
Jacket illustration and interior chapter spot illustrations
copyright © 2013 by Richard Cowdrey
Jacket designed by Karin Paprocki
For information about special discounts for bulk purchases, please contact
Simon & Schuster Special Sales at 1-866-506-1949
or business@simonandschuster.com.
The Simon & Schuster Speakers Bureau can bring authors to your live event. For
more information or to book an event contact the Simon & Schuster Speakers
Bureau at 1-866-248-3049 or visit our website at www.simonspeakers.com.
Interior designed by Hilary Zarycky
The text of this book was set in Yana.
Manufactured in the United States of America 0913 FFG
2 4 6 8 10 9 7 5 3 1
Library of Congress Control Number 2013933921
ISBN 978-1-4424-8638-6 (hc)
ISBN 978-1-4424-8637-9 (pbk)
ISBN 978-1-4424-8681-2 (eBook)

Chapter 1

HEN THE SUN APPEARED the blackbird began to sing. He was only a dark speck on the topmost branch of a tall and sturdy oak. Yet his singing floated through the forest and spread good cheer like a joyful reveille.

Pheasants, beating their wings loudly, swung down from their sleeping-trees. Their sharp clucks rang clear and metallic in the morning air. The woodpecker started his gay drumming, the magpies began their chattering and the titmice whispered softly in the underbrush.

The golden ball of the sun rose into the sky that was now turning a pale blue.

Perri the squirrel popped out of her nest. Waving her fire-red tail, she hurried from branch to branch. Then suddenly she sat still to listen to a blackbird. He sang on melodiously, his voice a delicate fluting that rose again and again in fresh cascades of song.

Even the roes lifted their heads to hear his carol. For them it meant that food, till now so sparse, would soon sprout in abundance. Tufts of their winter-bleached fur peeled off on the hawthorn, mulberry and hazel bushes as they slipped into the thicket.

At the forest's edge crouched a hare, pricking up first one ear, then the other. He peered about him, worried, frightened; both ears pointed yearningly across the little meadow. Mistrustful, he did not dare come out into the open, for the hares were always afraid. At night they feared the murderous claws of the owl, by day the hawk and the buzzard. Both night and day they fled from the stalking fox and the small but even more bloodthirsty weasel.

In the thicket, free of all fear, Tambo the great deer paused on his way to the bed where he rested during the day. For a short time he gave himself up to enjoying the birds' song, for he, too, longed for spring. He, too, sensed the encouraging approach of warmer days. The first growth of his antlers stirred a gentle fever in his blood.

A pair of young does had made loud frightened sounds when he had first appeared. Tambo watched them scamper off, and felt annoyed by their timidity, as he always did. He shook his head in bewilderment and with noiseless steps went along the path worn through the forest by his ancestors. Suddenly, not far from the trail, the leafless branches of a sapling quaked. Tambo stopped for a cautious look.

He saw a strong roebuck, already wearing his red summer coat. From the tips of his antlers the skin cover he was shedding hung in tatters. Strips of bark flew down from a young spruce and the bared wood shone white as the roebuck polished his horns.

Tambo watched him with approval and thought,

"That fellow's all right. He's got sense. I'll go talk with him. We'll be friends."

But he had hardly taken a step when the roebuck gave a cry of fright, then leaped aside angrily and broke away through the brushes.

Tambo's large, kind eyes grew dark and sad. "No use! They won't have anything to do with me!"

He continued on his way to the hollow which was his sleeping place. A heavy thicket fenced it in. He let himself down slowly. Hardly a movement of the bushes betrayed his presence.

Perri came and whispered, "Rest easy. I'll be on watch." The magpie flew to him and balanced on a branch, promising, "I'll report even the slightest danger."

Tambo nodded gratefully. He knew he could count on his sentries.

He would have liked to talk with the lively squirrel and the wise magpie about how shy the roes were toward him. He had often been at the point of mentioning this coolness, which he could not understand. He wanted an explanation very badly. Yet he could never bring himself to talk about it. He was ashamed because they seemed to shun him.

Gently he laid his head on the ground, moved his chin back and forth several times and then fell asleep.

The sun warmed the forest, gradually drank up the dew that sparkled like a million diamonds, and summoned all life to renewal. In answer the grass sprouted with vigor, violets opened their dark blue eyes, lilies of the valley awoke and moved their leaves like long listening ears. Ants scurried busily in the jungle of the turf. Butterflies unfolded their wings to dance playfully in the air. Tiny insects explored, bumblebees buzzed.

Juicy buds appeared on the bushes, so many that it seemed a green veil had been flung over the brown branches. As if by magic, the trees let their foliage emerge. Though still tiny, gay buds clustered on every branch of the chestnuts, oaks and birches, and on the firs new light-green needles breathed a spicy perfume.

The fragrance drawn forth by the sun's warmth was wonderfully varied and exciting. From the forest floor rose the sturdy smell of the wood of the trees, bursting with sap. From the blades of grass and from the flowers streamed waves of good clean odors and impulses of eager new life.

Martin had been perched for hours on the high platform of his lookout and could not rouse himself to leave. He had watched day come, had seen the sun rise into the heavens and the sky change from pale gray to light yellow, to shimmering green, and to the flame of the dawn. He had watched the does grazing in the meadow, Tambo the stag, the hares, the darting weasels, the awkwardly galloping hedgehogs, the slinking foxes. He had been moved to joy by the blackbirds' song. The chattering of the magpies and clucking of the pheasants had put him in a glad mood.

He looked close about him, then peered into the distance. This sea of treetops was his property, his world. It always brought him happiness.

Finally he climbed down and passed along the narrow uphill path to his house, the Forest Lodge. It stood in the middle of a large garden against the foot of the hillock. In the upper corner of the parklike acre was the stable.

Martin loved the isolation which the Lodge gave him. His only human companions were his old forester Peter and Peter's wife Babette. They were enough for Martin. For these two, who had served his parents before him and had watched over him since his childhood, were his friends. Solitary life was no hardship for him; and now that he could hardly remember when he had first chosen it, it had become a matter of course. The hump on his back, and the teasing and mockery that his deformity had drawn upon him as a schoolboy, had made him prefer to be alone. Here in the Lodge he lived completely unnoticed by the world. In this quietness of his own choosing, now so familiar, he was well satisfied.

He was never lonely here. The creatures in the stable, as well as those in the forest, had to be tended and cared for. Together they made a wide circle of friends, rich in variety because of the differences in their natures. Above all Martin loved them because they did not make fun of his ugliness, because they were simple and honest and completely free of the cruelty and guile and bitter ridicule that he had found in so many of his own kind.

As he walked toward the stable now, both his horses came out to meet him: Devil the fiery black stallion and Witch the fox-red mare. They could leave the stable whenever they wanted to; a gentle push on the swinging door and they were outside. They came ambling freely through the garden, lured forth by the golden spring day and by the sight of their two-legged friend.

Manni the donkey, who had been frisking in the garden, trotted over too to greet Martin. Insistently he pushed his long face close to Martin's humped chest to be scratched. He lowered his head with pleasure when his master softly stroked the space between his ears. When Martin paused as if he meant to stop, Manni grunted and pushed his head up again, wanting the petting to go on. Martin kept it up for some time, but finally said, "That's enough now, Manni," and the donkey at once moved aside.

Lisa the cow also came forward at Martin's call, and he patted her broad haunches. She drew off with apparent indifference, but in reality she was shy because she was going to have a calf. She was rigidly plump, and almost clumsy in her gait.

Martin stood lovingly by the horses, feeling the silky gentleness of their lips, looking into the dark beauty of their wise eyes. Vigorously he slapped the shining coat of their necks and backs. These animals from his stable made him just as happy as the wild inhabitants of the forest. He was at ease with them all.

At length he turned to walk back to the Lodge. Manni followed him to the very door and received a farewell fondling as reward.

When the donkey returned to the garden, Devil the stallion neighed at him, "You're always so forward!"

"Forward?" Manni repeated, looking thoughtful. He said nothing for a long time—Devil was always scolding him and trying to start a quarrel—but finally he came to a conclusion. "And *you* are stupid," he told Devil.

"Do you mean *me*?" the stallion burst out.

"You got that much anyhow," the donkey retorted.

Devil came up to him angrily. "You've got nerve! I'd like to show you just once."

"Show me what?" Manni asked innocently. "I'd like to see."

Witch the mare intervened. "Don't get in a row, please! We have such a wonderful life here. You two ought to be good friends."

Hesitating, Devil mumbled, "I only want to frighten the fresh little nitwit."

"Well, you haven't succeeded," Manni said stolidly. "Besides, I'm not the one who picks the quarrels."

"There he goes again!" Devil muttered.

Calm and unperturbed, Manni declared, "But, my excitable friend, you started it."

"Oh, well–" Devil's tone showed that he wanted to make up. "Are we friends or not?"

"Of course we're friends"–the donkey grinned–"because I'm so patient when you fly off the handle."

"There you go insulting me again!" cried the stallion.

"Oh, don't take it so hard," the donkey soothed him. "After all, can't I merely express my opinion?"

The stallion threw back his proud head, "Must you *always* have the last word?"

"And you the first?"

A loud sigh from the cow interrupted them. "Who cares about me?" Lisa complained.

"What's the matter?" Witch asked her in concern.

"I'm so afraid," Lisa quavered, "so afraid."

"Why?"

"For my baby."

"You needn't be afraid for it, you silly creature," the stallion threw in. "When the time comes, you'll have your baby and then the matter will be settled."

Lisa contradicted him. "No, not settled. . . ."

"Nonsense," Devil exclaimed. "Other mothers bring youngsters into the world. You act as if you were the first one, the only one."

"That's not what bothers me." The cow lowered her head and blew her breath out heavily.

"Then speak up," Witch urged her. "What *are* you so upset about?"

"They may take my baby. It's my first. Maybe they'll take it away from me."

Outraged, the stallion began to puff. "*Who'll* take

your baby from you? I? The Fiery One here? Or this Gray? None of us would even think of such a thing."

"The two-legged ones," moaned Lisa. "They will take my baby."

The donkey crossed over to her. "Now how did you get that idea? All by yourself?"

Tearfully Lisa looked at Manni. "No, I didn't get it by myself at all. My sisters and my other relatives told me. They all had it happen to them. When one of us bears a calf, she can't be happy with it. The Hes steal the beloved little one away from the mother. Nothing does any good. No use pleading or resisting. They drag the poor baby off. 'That's the way it will be with you,' they told me, 'so be prepared.' But I'm not prepared. I'm afraid. I can't bear to think of it."

"And what do the Hes do with your calves?" Manni wanted to know.

"They kill them."

"*Kill* them!" exclaimed Manni. "Why?"

Shaken with horror, Lisa choked out, "The Hes gobble up our murdered little ones."

"*Eat* them? Impossible!" Manni insisted, but he shuddered.

Witch, too, was trembling. She stamped, to hide her emotion. "Impossible!"

The donkey found words again. "*Our* two-legged friends here certainly don't do that. Perhaps such gruesome things do occur somewhere. Perhaps. Though I doubt even that. Maybe other Hes . . . but *ours* couldn't do such a thing." He shook his head emphatically. "You've got to believe that ours are not that sort."

The stallion whispered in Manni's ear, "And do you really know them so well?"

Manni retorted quickly, "Yes, I know them through and through," and turned back to Lisa. "I'll *prove* to you that they would never do such a thing."

"All right, prove it," Devil challenged. "Show me."

"Then don't interrupt," the donkey snorted. "Listen. You all know—don't you?—that our younger He never kills and the older He only kills in the forest out of mercy—to protect the innocent and to end suffering. And I've seen the dead creatures brought here, and *never* has there been a young one killed. Never! Not a single time have I seen a young one brought back. Isn't that proof? It shows they spare the young—even the wild ones. And they spare the mothers too." He faced Lisa. "You can trust me. And you can trust them too!"

Only half-reassured, the cow sighed, "If only you're right . . . if only my baby *does* stay with me. . . ." She turned and lumbered into the barn. "I must lie down now."

They could hear her slip carefully to the floor and then sigh deeply.

"You're really dumb, my friend," the donkey told the stallion.

Devil shook himself. "Dumb! You think you're the only one that's smart around here, I suppose. You're fresh—that's all."

"I don't know whether I'm smart or not," Manni declared, "but I know it was mighty dumb of you to pretend to be so wise and then air your doubts and get the poor girl more upset than ever."

The stallion galloped away rudely instead of answering.

Witch whispered to the donkey: "He doesn't mean any harm. But it was good you told him. He certainly needs a lesson." And, as if ashamed of her moment's disloyalty, she cantered off after the stallion.

Chapter 2

THE MOON HUNG HIGH IN THE clear heaven. Gradually the stars grew fainter and by and by went out. Only the evening star still sparkled like a fiery jewel, competing with the moonlight well into the first hours of the new morning.

Yet even when day was still far off, a sweet song sounded from aloft. Tirelessly the charming voice exulted, telling the end of darkness and welcoming the approach of light.

It was the voice of the lark.

Of all creatures the humble lark awakens first. Long before the rooster crows, even before the blackbird begins his morning tune, the lark sings of her happy life. She rises from her nest in the fields, swings high into the air, a tiny, almost invisible dot—a pinpoint of melody, pouring her song richly, zestfully, down toward the earth.

Under a tightly woven shelter of fir branches, Martin sat without moving. Enchanted, he listened to the lark and patiently awaited the coming of the heath cocks.

"Shioo—sheed!"

There one came, swishing down to the edge of the field.

"Shioo—sheed!"

A second, a third, a fourth, a fifth—Martin could not count all that gathered. He heard only their wings beating the air as they landed on their mating ground.

At once they began their courtship dance, turning and bowing, uttering their monotonous *"lu-lu-lu-lu—lu-lu-lu-lu."*

As the sky slowly grew brighter, they leaped at each

other, pair by pair, breast to breast, forward and back. Their threatening beaks were wide open and hissing. Their wings hung loose as they danced, and they lifted them just a little off the ground in short, quick, violent movements. Finally they fell back to the forest floor and resumed their peaceful but hurried rivalry and their *"lu-lu-lu-lu!"* They twisted and turned like whirling dervishes. The feathers covering their tails on either side now spread out. They faced each other with bodies arched like scythes while the protruding red glands over their eyes swelled brighter and brighter.

Martin had brought no gun to shoot them with. He had come as spectator, and had no idea of cutting short the delightful performance. He held a pair of field glasses to his eyes to bring the company of birds closer to him. Through the magic lenses he watched the hens parade before the milling ranks of dancers and fighters, the excited cocks. The hens behaved like ladies who watch eagerly for attention, pretending indifference but thrilled at heart.

Martin was amazed by the performance of one of

the dozen cocks–the smallest, who acted as if he were charged with high explosive. He called much louder than the others and leaped about more violently. Foolhardily he chased the others away from him until finally none dared approach. The glands shone from his forehead as if ready to burst. His eyes glittered like dark burning balls and his black tail feathers were as bright as metal.

As the sun appeared and sent out its first gentle rays, a heath hen flew up toward the forest. Instantly the smallest cock fluttered after her and then the entire band scattered, vanishing among the high trees singly or in pairs.

Now again Martin the hunchback heard the jubilant song of the lark sounding from the skies.

After a few more days of spring, the birds of passage returned from the south. First of all came the wild geese, in orderly wedgelike squadrons, one above the other. They flew in the evenings and in the dawns toward their home in the north. By day they generally rested on the banks of streams, sentries providing security by constant watchfulness. But here in the rolling country they hardly ever stopped. They only floated by, wedge after wedge in the clear sky. The freedom song of these wanderers rang down inspiringly from high above.

Martin loved the wild geese, loved to gaze at their wide, open formations that always etched the same three-cornered line in the moonlit or early-morning air. Thrilled, he listened to their triumphant call.

Sometime later the swallows arrived. It was their chirping and rustling that gave definite promise spring was really coming. Their darting and dipping was like a mischievous game filling the world above the trees with gaiety.

The trees of the forest and those in Martin's garden now put out tender green foliage. Bushes were decorated with buds. The grass of the fields and meadows grew faster. The blooms of violet, dandelion, crocus and hepatica strewed the green turf with rich color and fragrance. The sloe flowered and in the garden the forsythia showed yellow petals motionless in the still air.

Bumblebees, wasps, soft-winged beetles, countless shining flies buzzed around.

Through the forest the cuckoo sent his quiet throaty giggle. Restlessly the golden oriole swung from tree to tree singing his poem of joy without pause. "I am he-ere!"

In vain the jay bade him with loud screeches to be quiet: "Oh, shut up!" But the oriole paid no heed. The jay imitated his singing as he had already mimicked the blackbird's, the finch's, the dove's. Annoyed and confused, the oriole kept quiet for a few moments. Immediately the blackbird made friends with him. She whispered, "Tell me about those countries where there's always summer. Tell me about the great water you crossed."

But the oriole's answer was only, "Oh, yes, I am he-ere!" He hurled himself into the air and flew to the next tree.

The blackbird sat alone. Then she searched the nearby branches until she found the nightingale. She asked her the same questions.

The nightingale replied softly, "The water doesn't frighten me. I cross it quickly, and find sunny lands with wonderful food."

"Then why does none of you stay there—not a single one—if it's so beautiful?"

"Stay there?" The nightingale was amazed. "How would that be possible? We have to come back here. This is our homeland. There we're just visitors."

"My ancient ancestors," explained the blackbird, "once upon a time also took these journeys. But their descendants, their grandchildren and great-grandchildren, loved their homeland so much they didn't want to wander any more. We became unused to travel. Now we stay here even when it's very cold. I think it's a pity."

Soon all began eagerly to build their nests. The lark, always first to awaken, was also first to return home and fashion her simple nest on the ground. The others, singing and twittering happily, built new homes or freshened up those they had left in the fall. Artfully the swallows attached their nests to the eaves of Martin's house, so close under that they could barely slip into them.

Manni the donkey spoke to the little birds. "Welcome, gallant fliers!"

"Greetings! Greetings!" the swallows chirped and

swished hastily away to fetch new building material.

"Why do you make your doors so tight?" the donkey wanted to know when they came back.

"No time to talk now!" the swallows shouted and were off again.

"Don't disturb them in their work," Lisa the cow reproved him gently.

Devil the stallion muttered, "Now don't you mix into this. Who are you to give orders to the Gray One?"

"Are you dictating to me?" Lisa asked him calmly. "You know I'm not afraid of you. After all, I can give Gray a piece of advice without asking your permission."

"What kind of advice?" Manni inquired.

"I mean," said Lisa, "it's better to wait till the little flycatchers are on the way to hatching. Then the parents sit quietly and are glad to talk to you."

"You're right," Manni admitted good-naturedly. "That's sensible."

Placidly the stallion said, "Yes, this time she's right. But it's an exception. Usually the milk-giver is really stupid, as dumb as the oats we eat. And *I'm* right about that."

The donkey turned to go.

"You needn't run away," neighed the stallion.

"I'm not running away," answered Manni. "I just want to take a look at the forest."

"The forest! You're crazy!" Devil exclaimed.

"But I've never been in the forest," the donkey brayed stubbornly. "I want to see what it's like."

"But suppose He needs you!" Witch the mare called after him.

Manni hesitated only a second. For a long time he had wanted to see the forest. Now he was determined to go. "Let Him—" What he was going to say trailed off into nothing as he pushed through the stable door.

"Gray has declared his independence," muttered the stallion.

"Only for this once," Witch said as if to apologize for Manni.

Lisa kept wagging her head in amazement. "None of us barn creatures belongs in the forest! How can he dare do such a thing?"

Chapter 3

ANNI AVOIDED HIS USUAL path to the Lodge. Softly he stole around the stable to where the ground rose and only the picket fence separated the garden from the hill. He had often stood there to glance longingly upward, only to do a timid about-face and stay home after all.

But today he was filled with the adventurous spirit of spring, its freshness and courage, though he didn't know it. He fancied that the courage overpowering his conscience came entirely from within himself.

As he stood there laying bold plans, a brilliant butterfly tumbled in the air before his eyes. Admiringly Manni followed him as he danced up and down the length of the fence. When at last the fragment of color flew off into the forest, Manni pressed through the little gate that was always unfastened.

The way went steeply uphill. Vigorously Manni climbed higher and higher. The brush pressed around him, the young shoots on the branches tempted his taste. High above his head the treetops interlaced to form a leafy green ceiling. He did not feel tired until he reached a clearing at the top. There he rested and drew deep breaths.

Suddenly he heard a thin peevish voice asking over and over: "Who are you? Tell us, who are you?"

Manni looked around. A squirrel came darting through the trees, a streak of red amid the green. She stopped on a low branch, flirted her bushy flag and complained, "Can't you hear me? I asked you who you are!"

"Oh, probably you've never been to our place down in the garden," Manni answered politely. "Otherwise you'd know me."

"Garden?" repeated Perri. "What's that? And where is it?"

"Down there where the forest stops. It's a piece of land. All the trees are cared for, and the bushes too. And He plants flower beds among them. You'd like it there."

The little squirrel laughed. "Oh, no, I wouldn't. I don't like any place but this. How'd you ever happen to come up to the forest?"

"Oh, I–I just wanted to–"

"You stutter and mumble so!" the squirrel interrupted. "Ah! *Now* I know who you are. You're the stupid one! The big stupid!"

The donkey opened his eyes wide in hurt surprise. "You're wrong, my little friend. Let me tell you–"

But Perri had already scampered up the tree and disappeared.

Manni broke farther through the thicket. The beauty of the forest took his mind from his hurt feelings. "Why, it's magnificent here!" he thought.

Suddenly he halted. Two roe deer sprang up in fright and bounded off. They were soon out of sight. All he could hear was their frightened *Ba-uh!* He thought, "Funny—they're afraid of me! I'd have liked to talk with them. And they're red, too, like the little tree-dancer. It seems everybody in the forest is red."

"Oh, ye-es! Who-o is he-ere?" exulted the oriole above his head.

Manni stopped short again, for he felt obliged to answer. "It's I," he said, but only in a small voice lest he frighten another creature away.

Paying no attention, the oriole kept up his glad shouting. "Who is he-ere? I am he-ere!"

Manni caught sight of the lovely bird throwing himself in short jerky flights from treetop to treetop.

"What a wonderful yellow he is—as if he'd been dipped in sunshine!" thought the donkey, standing still amid thick bushes in order to see the happy ball of feathered color again.

Closer to him, a magpie alighted on a hazel bush

and the branch swung to and fro a little. When Manni turned to her, the magpie started in alarm.

The donkey asked politely, "Do you know that mad singer up there?"

Reassured, the magpie cackled sarcastically: "The yellow one? Why shouldn't I know him? But I'm meeting *you* now for the first time. What are you after?"

"Nothing," Manni replied, "nothing, really. You needn't be afraid of me. I'm not going to hurt anybody."

"Well, well!" mocked the magpie. Just by way of caution she sought a perch somewhat higher. "That's what the red robber says, too."

"Red!" The word slipped off Manni's tongue. "Who's he? Almost everyone here is red."

The magpie ignored the interruption. "How'd you get here? And what did you come for?"

Embarrassed, the donkey tried to explain. "I wanted—well, I don't live far away. With Him—"

"With Him, eh?" Interested now, the magpie came nearer. "Well, He's good! And He doesn't do us any harm. Now if I could only trust you . . ."

"You can trust me," Manni said.

"Some other time," the magpie cackled. "You're too big, too heavy. Safe is safe!" And she flew swiftly away.

"Now why did she do that?" the donkey said to himself. "That blue-winged simpleton thinks I'm a robber. The silly little thing!"

Manni trotted farther. He didn't know that to move without sound is the law of the wild. He went very noisily, chewing occasionally on the leaves of bushes that reached out to him. "It's wonderful in the forest—wonderful!" he thought. "I'd come here often if my duties—if He would let me."

The bushes rustled. Tambo appeared, huge and powerful, his tall branching crown lowered with hostile purpose. Without realizing it, Manni had come to the stag's resting place and awakened him out of his sleep.

Amazed, the donkey stuttered, "I—I—won't hurt you!"

"That's what robbers always say," Tambo muttered with annoyance. "And there's no one who'd dare pick on me except you."

"But I'm not trying to pick a fight with you! Let's

be friends instead." The donkey spoke sincerely. But Tambo's clear, deep eyes examined him and Manni found it hard to bear up under the regal stare. "Believe me—please believe me—I'd like to be your friend," he begged. "I like you very much."

"Well, I don't like you at all," retorted Tambo, his forelegs moving restlessly. Suddenly he lifted one slender leg and slashed at Manni with the sharp hoof.

The donkey hastily backed away, trembling. "Why do you hate me so?"

Tambo saw Manni's shivering, and said quietly, "It was a long while ago, so long that none of my forebears could remember it, but it's been handed down to us that once on a time bloodthirsty monsters lived here. We had to wage a constant life-and-death struggle with them."

"What did they look like?" asked Manni.

"I don't know," Tambo said. "They were all killed by Him ages ago. Maybe they looked like you."

The donkey forced a laugh. "If they looked like me, then they certainly weren't dangerous!"

Tambo answered, "That's what you'd say, of course." His dark eyes looked carefully at Manni again. "One must think of every possibility. But I see what you mean."

Relieved that danger seemed to have passed, Manni tore a few leaves from a tree. He chewed them eagerly, partly because he was hungry, partly because he wanted to convince the stag of his harmlessness.

In a surprised and changed tone Tambo asked, "Do you like to eat that sort of thing, too?"

"I've never tasted this before," Manni replied. "It's no delicacy, at least not for me. At home I'm served far better stuff."

"What, for instance?" inquired Tambo, still a bit mistrustful.

"Hay, oats, sweet corn, and all kinds of fresh green things."

"Where is your home?" the stag asked with growing interest.

"Down there with Him. I work for Him," Manni stated proudly.

"Him," Tambo repeated in a more friendly tone. "Aren't you afraid of Him?"

"Why should I be? He's good to me, and to the horses and the cow. He's good to all creatures," Manni bragged.

"Remarkable!" But Tambo inspected the donkey with dawning respect. "And don't you ever get anything alive to eat?"

"Ugh!" The donkey snorted in disgust. "We eat only what grows out of the ground, never anything else."

"Then–" Tambo came closer–"then we can be friends."

Manni asked happily, "Well then, tell me, my new friend, are *you* afraid of Him?"

Tambo's head lifted majestically. "Afraid is not the right word. I–I avoid Him. His scent makes me uneasy. Besides, I don't know Him very well. But I'm afraid of no one, and no one dares come near me."

"I can understand that," the donkey agreed. "You're big and strong. Perhaps only the horses are bigger and stronger."

"Horses? I don't know them."

"Don't worry. They're very nice. With their strength they can carry Him and run at the same time. I can carry Him too and run, of course. But not so fast or so long."

"I'd like to see a horse."

"They'd be frightened of your antlers, just as I am—*was*, I mean."

"My crown? Oh, yes. It's only just growing." Tambo was haughty yet modest.

"Growing?" Manni echoed wonderingly. "It looks fully grown to me. And very stately."

"No, it's still sprouting. There's no mistake about it, for this is my fifth."

"What! Where are the others?" Manni felt as if he were hearing a fairy tale.

"They fell off," explained Tambo. "Every year at the end of winter my crown falls off. Every year in the spring it grows again, always bigger and stronger."

"Doesn't it hurt you—falling off that way and growing again?"

"I hardly feel the loss of the old crown. My head becomes lighter. For a time I'm afraid I won't be able to defend myself. But the new growth gives me a wonderful feeling of courage and power."

The donkey could only say, "Lucky fellow!"

"Now you'll excuse me. I want to sleep some more," Tambo said, "so good-by!" He lowered himself and appeared to doze immediately.

He did not even seem to hear Manni's respectful "Good-by!"

Going on his way the donkey mused, "What a noble creature! What a fine, free life he leads." Richer with experience now, Manni thought reluctantly of returning home. "My old friends will be wondering about me—the rough one, the gentle one and the milk-giver. How amazed they'll be when I tell them my adventure— when I describe the loveliness of the forest, the exciting happenings and my talk with the wearer of the crown."

A pheasant strutted serenely by. His head bobbing, he pulled at grasses and herbs and seemed not at all afraid of Manni.

The donkey looked at him with amazement. "What a handsome bird! Oh, that shimmering neck–"

Manni started in fresh surprise as a hare sat up before him. The hare's whiskers vibrated with busy sniffing.

"Greetings, little friend," the donkey addressed him. "Did I wake you up?"

"Greetings," whispered the hare. "Wake me up? Oh, no. I mustn't sleep. I can hardly ever sleep. I must always protect myself!"

"Why?" Manni asked sympathetically.

The hare suddenly pricked up his ears, darted between the legs of the startled donkey and sped off. Manni turned his neck to stare after the wildly fleeing fellow, only to see him disappear.

A sharp scent penetrated the donkey's nostrils. Before he could gather his wits there was a violent snapping of small branches and a fox came loping through the underbrush. The pheasant screeched and tried to fly, but too late. The fox fell on the back of his prey, pressing the bird flat to the ground. His bared teeth bit hard into the pheasant's neck.

Manni was terribly frightened by the scream of the pheasant. He saw the wings jerk wide and helpless, saw blood gush from the fatal wound. He tried to control his horror.

"You treacherous murderer!" he cried.

But the fox glared back at him, his jowls drawn up so that his teeth could be seen. "You fool!" he snarled. "You stupid grass-eater! Don't you know what hunger is? Get away! Interfere with me and you'll be sorry!"

The hair on Manni's back rose. He stared hypnotized at the raving red animal.

The fox completed the kill and then yapped at the donkey, "Did you understand? I said get out of here!"

Manni fled, speeded by the horror of what he had seen. The rank odor of the fox stayed in his nostrils. He was trembling. "Enough!" he told himself. "I've had enough of the forest–the murderous forest!"

He ran faster and faster, his galloping a flight. When he reached the gate and saw the garden, the roofs of the house and the barn, he breathed a deep sigh of relief.

Chapter 4

I S MARTIN PORING OVER HIS BOOKS again?" Babette, the forester's wife, inquired.

"No," old Peter reported. "He's sketching."

"Where is he?"

"In the barn or somewhere around."

"Call him in. He must eat something."

"When he wants to eat, he'll come in of his own accord."

"What a way to live!" sighed Babette good-humoredly, pushing back her fluffy gray hair. "Always alone."

"But that's what he prefers," Peter said.

"I know. He really never feels lonely at all." Babette sighed again. "How often we've said these same things...." She brushed her eyes with the back of her hand. "Ever since that time when he was still a schoolboy—you remember, Peter. When he came trudging up from school, after the children had teased him so. His father and mother dead, poor lamb, and he a poor orphan with a hump on his back—and those children teasing and making fun of him.... Oh, Peter, no wonder he said he never wanted to see any human being again. Only the two of us—"

The strongly built old man put his arm around her. "But he's happy now. He loves his animals. They give him confidence for confidence, faithfulness for faithfulness, love for love. Remember that! Don't feel sad for him, he doesn't need it. He's really happy with his forest beasts and birds, and his animals in the barn."

Babette nodded, wiping her eyes. "Yes—you're right. He's made a little world for himself here in the forest."

"It doesn't seem so small to me," Peter smiled.

"Don't forget, the sun and the stars are his friends too."

While they were talking, Martin the hunchback was sitting on a stool near the garden with his drawing board on his knees, trying to sketch the heath cocks from memory. The horses lazed around him. Now and then Devil would look over Martin's shoulder or Witch would rest her long jaw on his arm. This made Martin happy, for to him it meant that his animal friends accepted him as he was and did not mind his ugliness. He reached back to caress the soft velvet of Witch's nose. Lisa, however, avoided him. She stood looking at him from a distance.

"What's the matter with you?" Martin called to her. He took a handful of salt out of a pouch to lure her. But she stood still.

Martin arose. "Why are you so shy?" He went toward her. She retreated on clumsy legs. He laughed softly. "So! Your condition. That's why you're nervous. Now I understand."

His soft voice had a soothing effect. Lisa stopped. He offered her the salt. She blew into his hand and licked the briny delicacy with her tongue.

Devil and Witch ambled up and both whispered to Lisa, "Don't be afraid of Him. He won't do you any harm."

Martin's free hand gently stroked Lisa's forehead. "Be patient, good girl. You'll soon have your calf."

As if she had understood every word and suddenly remembered her dread, Lisa made a frightened leap sidewise and trotted stiffly away. Martin looked after her, shaking his head and murmuring, "What's the matter with her *now?*"

It was just then that Manni came home from the forest. He caught sight of Martin and ran happily to him to rub his head against his chest.

Martin scratched his long-eared friend's throat. "Hello, old fellow. Where have you been?"

Manni wished he could tell Martin his experiences. He looked with gentle sorrow into Martin's eyes and received in return a kindly gaze in which too there was something of sadness.

Martin gathered together his drawing board and pencils. "See you again, my friends," he said. The horses and Manni went with him to the house door.

Once the animals were alone, the horses showered the donkey with questions. "What was it like in the forest? What did you do there?"

Manni didn't answer.

Devil neighed, "Answer me! We know only the wide roads where He rides. Answer us! How is it up there?"

Manni jolted off stubbornly. Once he had dreamed of telling them his adventures but now when the opportunity came he grew obstinate. That was his funny way. The stallion and the mare overtook him quickly.

"Behave!" the stallion admonished him. "Show some manners."

"I always do," Manni said innocently.

"You don't! You're ridiculous!"

"Think so?" The donkey grinned.

Witch pleaded, "At least tell us what you—"

Manni interrupted her. "You know the forest. You've been up there often. Why ask me?"

"Up there, up there!" said Devil heatedly. "We never go up there except when we have to carry Him."

"And He rides only in the wide clearings and on the few big roads," Witch added.

"And you," said Devil, "probably cut right across?"

"Of course," Manni retorted. "I don't do it down here in the garden any more than you do. But up there I cut right through the middle of the thicket."

"I knew it!" The stallion showed his burning curiosity. "Now tell us!"

"Yes, tell us!" Witch urged.

"What should I say?" The donkey spread his front legs and held his willful head cocked high. "Up there one's a foreigner, and by no means welcome!"

The stallion stamped. "Go on, go on!"

"There's nothing more!" Manni teased him.

"Oh, there must be," begged the mare. "Tell us!"

The donkey gave in a little–just enough to tantalize. "There's no trace of our safe and peaceful existence up there."

"No safety?" Devil was surprised.

"No peace?" marveled Witch.

Disgustedly Manni bared his teeth. "Not a trace of it!

Some commit murder, others are murdered. I wouldn't like to live up there." He threw himself into the grass and rolled over. "It's so good here. This is still the most beautiful place. Well, now I won't say any more! Leave me alone. I want peace!"

"Oh, *please* tell us what you saw," implored Witch.

Manni rolled over on his back, all four legs in the air, and grumbled lazily, "Later, maybe. Later ... sometime ..."

Martin could see barely more than three paces ahead, for darkness still shrouded the trees. But it was no longer night and not yet day.

He liked this in-between time best. He sensed a wonderful mystery in this hour of vanishing night and wakening day. At such a time the turning of the globe seemed to him like the turning of fate, like a delivery from darkness and anxiety to happiness and courage.

He crossed a small clearing. Giant oaks rustled, the shadow of their tops spreading wide. In the gloaming four slender birches stood out silvery and clear.

Martin re-entered the forest on a narrow trail that snaked its way through the underbrush.

Nearby stood a doe, her newborn kid beside her. She stiffened to attention, ears quivering. Her sharp hearing had caught Martin's almost inaudible step. The kid listened too, its legs braced ready to leap away. The mother roe calmed her child. "Don't be afraid. There's no need to run away. It's He! He never hurts us."

The oak trees began to talk among themselves in soft whispers.

"Oh, times have been good since He has ruled here and while His father ruled before him. You young birches, you don't remember how it was before father and son protected the forest."

A young birch lisped, "Protected the forest? How?"

"What was there before?" another young one asked.

The old oak answered, "Never a day passed that the thunder-stick did not resound. At times the Hes came in crowds. Roes, stags, hares fell over and died. Even squirrels were knocked off our branches. What madness and what horrible shouting! All the forest residents were terrified. The thunder-sticks roared. And there were not only the thunder-sticks. The Hes carried great teeth also and in winter bit into stalwart trees with them so that the trees fell over. We ourselves were afraid of being bitten and losing our lives."

The third birch inquired, "This He who's here now—He does nothing harmful? Nothing at all?"

"No!" the oaks chorused. "Neither His father who used to be here, nor He. Nothing—nothing bad!"

"But He throws the thunder-stick," a birch called out.

"Only the older two-legged one does, the one with gray fur on his head," whispered the ancient oak. "And then but rarely. Very rarely. Really only to help us."

The strongest oak made himself heard. "When a stag or a doe falls by that thunder-stick, it is because he is past his time, ill and rotten as a tree which must fall soon. It is kindness then."

Martin could hear only the soft morning rustle of the forest. He understood the language of the trees no more than he understood the speech of the animals. Yet he had an instinctive feeling of oneness with other forms of life. This happy feeling swelled his misshapen chest so that he drew in his breath lightly and freely.

The growing light spread. The leaves and the sky took on a hue of delicate green.

Martin climbed to his lookout platform built in the shadow of a birch tree at the edge of a large meadow. From there he could see the green arch of the treetops and a tremendous sky in which the morning star was twinkling its farewell.

In the meadow three stags, with the horns still covered by their velvet, were grazing at ease. They strolled around in the manner of great gentlemen, nibbling a bit here and there or merely looking off into space for moments at a time.

Regretfully they glanced at a roe which they had scared into flight. "We wouldn't have done anything to him," said a stag whose horns had ten branches.

The youngest, who had only six branches, said, "Certainly not."

Tambo added, "When have we ever done anything

to one of these little fellows? They are relatives of ours. It's painful to see them avoid us."

The first stag stretched out his head in thought. His horns lay almost flat on his back. "My father," he recalled, "told me a story he heard from one of our forefathers. A long time ago a roebuck was speared by one of our ancient ancestors–in anger."

Tambo said, "During the mating season I too become angry at my own kind. At such times we all get angry."

"Even though they happen very seldom," continued the first stag, "such acts of violence live in the memory of our children and their children. It is not surprising that smaller ones are frightened at the mere sight of us and flee because of our power. Who would dare fight with one of us?"

"Do you feel a prickling in your crown as I do?" the six-pointer asked.

"A little," answered the ten-pointer.

Tambo said, "My crown isn't hard enough yet. But soon I'll rub it against the tree trunks."

They wandered apart, each sauntering by himself.

Tambo drifted toward the lookout, then stopped suddenly as he caught sight of Martin. After a few seconds he strolled quietly back to the other two and murmured, "Imagine! He is here!"

"That's nothing," the ten-pointer said. "He comes here every day."

But the young six-pointer grew excited. "Where? Where is He? I've never seen Him!"

The three stags stared upward at Martin. He found it the purest joy to have them watch him without fear.

"Can you see Him?" asked the ten-pointer of the youngest stag.

"Yes! He looks dreadful—dreadful!" The young deer stamped and nervously approached the platform. Curiosity made him bold, yet he was prepared for flight.

"He's not dreadful at all," Tambo retorted. "I know Him. You must get used to Him."

"No," whispered the six-pointer, "I couldn't. I can't bear that look of His!" And he leaped away into the thicket.

"Young and stupid and inexperienced," Tambo scoffed good-naturedly.

"It's time for us to go too," the ten-pointer urged.

"Well, let's go then. It's all right with me."

They moved away slowly, lifting their slender legs in proud mincing steps, nibbling here and there at the young shoots by the forest's edge. Finally they vanished into the wall of brush.

Martin watched their majestic departure with the keenest enjoyment. Then he turned his gaze over the green ocean of treetops toward the coming of the day.

In the sky the light green was giving way to a pale lemon-yellow. The yellow grew deeper and deeper until it was shot through by tongues of pink which in turn became streamers of flame. Martin witnessed the display with delight. No matter how often he saw this climax, its effect upon him was never less. Instead, from year to year it entranced him ever more.

Old Peter was in the barn milking the cow.

"Yes, Lisa. It won't be long before you're calving."

The brown cow turned her wide-browed head to him, a question in her large eyes.

Peter said again, "Yes, Lisa, soon. Very soon now."

The cow lowed softly.

"Now you can go out in the sun," Peter said. "It'll do you good."

Lisa moved off with her slow lumbering gait, stopping for a moment in the doorway. She managed a little leap over the doorsill and ambled off laboriously.

The Persian tomcat looked with interest at Peter who was pouring some milk out of the pail into a saucer on the floor. "There you are, Shah," Peter told him. "Your share."

The cat stepped up to the saucer with dignity. He sat down close to it and lapped daintily, with affectation but without greed.

"It takes people who can admire spirit to appreciate a cat," Peter thought. "That Shah is a free, wild creature. He doesn't allow himself to be ordered around. He defends himself, and he gives his friendship only to those who deserve it."

Out of the wall trough Peter fetched a small piece of raw meat which he had prepared beforehand. In a low inviting tone he called, "Gentle guest, where are you?"

From a dark corner up under the roof a great gray owl flew soundlessly down to perch on the partition dividing the stable. Though the clapping of her beak sounded threatening, her melancholy eyes were very soft. She took the little piece of meat cautiously.

"Is it good?" Peter asked. He waited until the owl swallowed the morsel, then picked her up and held her like a baby. Gently he scratched the delicate breast feathers. She seemed to enjoy the caress.

Peter thought how long it had been before the owl began to trust him and grew so tame that they could become friends. "A cat and an owl—" he said to himself; "they are both mysterious and both have dangerous enemies." He patted the bird in his arms again. Then he released her and she flew back to her hidden corner. When he went out of the barn with the milk pail, the Persian cat followed him, found a place in the sun and stretched out to sleep.

Chapter 5

TAMBO HAD RUBBED THE VELVET off his antlers, as the wise stags did every year.

He could not see how richly pearled they were, nor how their twelve points glistened like ivory. But he knew his crown was beautiful, and the knowledge filled him with pride and strength.

Ever since his birth he had acted in obedience to his inner urge. He did not understand this whispering of instinct, but he obeyed it faithfully. It had guided him while he had still been with his mother, and also after he had left her and had ranged around alone, a young stag with only the beginnings of horns. During the mating seasons of several years, too, these inner whisperings had told him that he must hide humbly from the Kings, and not arouse their jealousy by wooing does who belonged to the great stags' harems.

Finally had come his courageous struggle for self-assertion. At first he had been defeated by other stags, though by no means shamefully. He had never lost his confidence in himself and had known that some day soon he would conquer, once and for all. No longer timid, he continued to put forth his claim to rule.

In the next year, after a short but furious struggle, Tambo had wounded his opponent and put him to flight. And so the mighty warrior became the ruling stag. His boldly won position was not contested.

Now Tambo walked alone.

He came into the open only when darkness was complete and then only in out-of-the-way places. He grazed here and there, but never twice in succession in the same clearing or meadow. And he always sought the thicket before the first sign of dawn. It was a life he loved. He was not bored, for animals of the forest are never bored.

Like all other stags, but more luxuriously, Tambo lived chiefly to take good care of himself, to gather choice food and build up his fine strength. In doing these things, he obeyed his whispering instinct. His gift of keen scent became more sensitive than ever, his hearing sharper, his caution a highly perfected sense.

Now the frightened cries of the roe deer who sometimes crossed his path did not bother him at all. He ignored them and simply passed by, a true king of the forest. His slender legs firmly supported his full, taut torso with its sleek covering of red. From his neck hung a black mane, thickly matted with burrs and leaves picked up as he carelessly roamed through bush and thicket. Above towered the noble, high-crowned head with its bearing of reserved and majestic dignity. The calm dark eyes shone magnificently.

His chief companions were the birds and the squirrel who came to him sometimes for a chat, for Tambo was often awake even during the day. In midnight darkness the hoot owl would frequently visit him.

"Tambo! Tambo!" called the hoot owl one night. "Do I disturb you?"

"No, my little friend, I'm awake."

"Did I frighten you?"

"No. I heard you fly in."

Touched on a point of pride, the hoot owl plunged his crooked beak into the feathers of his breast. "Impossible! I fly without a sound."

"I can hear you just the same. Or maybe I hear only the air that your wings stir up."

"Maybe that's it." The hoot owl was quickly mollified. "It's a good thing the little fellows I hunt can't hear as well as you do. Of course they're usually asleep when I go after them. But even if they wake up, as some do, I'm on them before they know it. That's the way to handle your prey."

"Prey . . ." Tambo's slightly troubled gaze rested on the round featherball rocking on a branch. "Prey! It's not easy for me to imagine what that means."

The hoot owl giggled softly. "Prey, my dear fellow, is something that writhes and squeaks—something that gives you pleasure and fills you up."

"I'm filled up by leaves and herbs and grasses. I never kill anyone."

"You're foolish," croaked the other. "You with your pronged crown, and with your strength and great size—who could hold against you? Think of all you could catch!"

"I'm surrounded by plenty," said Tambo placidly. "I'm never hungry and I wouldn't care for such murderous 'pleasures.'" He turned quietly away. "Good night."

"Foolish giant!" mocked the hoot owl, and floated off to the treetops. "All giants are silly." He laughed to himself.

Tambo only half heard these words and paid no attention to them. Noiselessly he moved through the brush, his step halting whenever he caught the tiniest sound.

Suddenly he came to a stop. Another owl, the great gray owl, had just perched close to him.

"Greetings!" she whispered in her thin but pleasant voice.

"Greetings!" whispered Tambo, who preferred the big owl to the hoot owl.

The bird started the conversation. "You know I live with Him."

"What!" Tambo was gravely surprised. "You're friendly with Him?"

"Very intimate."

Tambo stared at her. "Aren't you afraid?"

"Afraid?" The owl's laughter sounded like a melancholy song. "Every day He calls me and I go to Him. He always has some tidbit for me."

"Mm, that's right," Tambo remembered. "In the winter He lays out sweet clover and piles of chestnuts for us."

"There! You see? He's good."

"Still," objected Tambo, "I can't help being afraid of Him. Not exactly afraid—but still—"

"Then you're very foolish. Why, I lie in His arms and let Him pet me. He knows just what kind of petting an owl likes best."

Tambo looked at the speaker as if he could hardly believe her. "Amazing!"

The owl began singing to herself in low crooning hoots, remembering happily. The sound made Tambo drowsy.

"I think I'll go to bed now," he said gently. "Good-by." He walked quietly away.

The owl sang him a friendly farewell and swung gracefully up into the air.

It was still long before day and quite dark. Tambo lay down to sleep, not in his accustomed bed but in a remote part of the underbrush. He slept, but only in snatches. Again and again he opened his eyes, pricked his ears, sniffed cautiously, and then dozed off once more.

When he finally arose the morning was far gone. Feeling hungry, he began to graze, but fastidiously, choosing only the delicate grasses.

Then he had another visitor. Near his lowered head, the woodpecker knocked on a poplar trunk. "Good day! Beautiful weather!" the cocky bird greeted. "And it's a good day for me because last night again no one caught me."

"Who would do anything to you?" scoffed Tambo.

The woodpecker laughed shrilly. "You're funny! Don't you know any great owls, any hoot owls, any martens?"

"They aren't all after you, are they?"

"Whether they're after *me* specially or not, I don't know. But if they can snap me up on the way it's all over for me just the same." He laughed bitterly. "So far they haven't had a chance at me, though. I hide too well."

"Aren't you afraid during the day?"

"Oh, much less then. Of course I must *always* be on guard." He flew higher, ending the chat without formality. He drummed and laughed aloud now and then.

Tambo dozed standing. But a shaking and chattering in the branches again brought him wide awake.

Perri the squirrel dashed down, nearly tumbling. She stopped suddenly with a raised flag of tail on a beech branch. "Greetings, powerful one!" she called. "Oh, lucky you! No one dares come near you, but *I* meet so many dangers."

"Who's after you now?" asked Tambo in concern.

"Oh, there's a robber at large in the forest! Nobody knows him. He's neither fox nor marten. But he climbs trees like a marten. I saw him! He just chased me. He's fast, but I'm much faster—lucky for me!" Perri bared her gnawing teeth.

"Too bad there must always be robbers," Tambo sighed. "Of course you're right that I needn't be afraid."

"But you act as if you were," Perri said saucily.

"Yes, I suppose I do," Tambo admitted. "But it's only caution. It's—I don't exactly know what. It's my nature to be wary. But I'm not afraid of robbers. I live peacefully and feed myself from the green plenty around us. I hate stealing and killing just as much as you do."

"Don't say that, powerful one." With her forepaw Perri wiped her face in momentary embarrassment, but then grew pert again. "Little birds taste wonderful. I just found some nests filled with—"

"I'd rather you didn't tell me such things," Tambo interrupted. "The forest would be heavenly without you fellows who kill to please your stomachs."

"Oh, you're mistaken, powerful one," laughed Perri. "Without us the forest would be boring. Nobody could stand such a dull life! The way things are—with danger, with the need for courage, with the sweet relief of escape, with the well-earned success of staying alive at all—*that's* why I love the forest!"

"It's a matter of taste," Tambo muttered uncomfortably.

"Nonsense! Even for you danger has charm. That 'caution' of yours—you enjoy it. You know you do!" Perri leaped impudently over the great stag and with flirting tail dashed up an oak trunk. "Farewell—powerful and *gentle* friend!"

Tambo fell to grazing. He started on a new round, moving alertly through the trees, browsing in search of something especially tasty. Often he slowed his progress to listen and to catch passing scents. He avoided making any sound.

There! A footfall, very soft, very stealthy. It was He, trying not to make the least noise!

Sudden fright shot through Tambo's great body,

dimming his sight and paralyzing his legs. He whirled clumsily and broke into a run.

Presently he stopped to catch his breath, for he realized he was hidden by heavy foliage. He could hear Him moving somewhere far off. And he heard his own heart beat.

Hoofbeats close by frightened him again, so violently that his rear legs trembled. He heard the soft padding and the panting of some smaller animal. Poor Tambo fell into terrible confusion. He ran senselessly in the same direction as the horse and dog trotting outside on the forest road. He was hidden from Martin, out on an innocent pleasure ride, only by the thicket and a thin wall of trees.

Then, like thunder roaring down out of a clear sky, a shot crashed.

The sound went through Tambo like a blow. His body lifted as if he had been hit by a bullet. He leaped to one side, dashing here and there blind with terror. He broke through hedges, and stopped with gasping chest only when a jay swooped in his path, fluttered around his nose and shouted at him with loud croakings:

"Be calm! Be calm, my friend! No danger!"

Tambo tried to conceal his trembling. He whispered in a low voice, "The thunder-stick—"

"The thunder-stick wasn't meant for you," the jay soothed him. "It fetched the marten down off the tree. That was the older He—the one with the gray fur on his head."

"And the galloping?" Tambo demanded, still anxious. "All that trampling—and the yapping?"

The jay smiled. "The younger He right over there behind the trees. He doesn't seem to have any thunder-stick at all. He rides only for enjoyment. Yes, on His horse. His dog runs along, just for fun too. All three of them are as innocent of any killing as you are."

"Are you sure?"

"I'm *very* sure." The jay spread his wings. "Farewell! I'll watch, and I'll warn you if it's necessary." He flew away.

Tambo breathed in deep relief. Perhaps the squirrel was right! The happiness of being safe burned fiercely in him. He glided back through the bush and the thicket without a sound.

He went on pondering what Perri had said, and now he was convinced. "Yes," he told himself, "it's beautiful in the forest just the way things are. For us they are as they should be!"

Chapter 6

IN THE EARLY-MORNING HOURS WHILE
it was still dark, Lisa began to groan. She groaned
softly at first, then louder and louder.

"Quiet!" neighed Devil.

But Lisa continued, always louder and more complaining.

"I want to sleep!" The stallion stamped. "Haven't you
any consideration? Be still!"

"Be still yourself!" retorted the donkey. "Don't you
know what's happening? The milk-giver is going to

have her baby. It's we who must have consideration for her."

The stallion fell silent.

Witch went over to Lisa. "Is the pain bad?"

"Yes, very bad," the cow replied. "And oh, I'm so worried."

Manni too had pushed into Lisa's stall. "Worried? Nonsense. You'll be all right."

"No, no—about my baby—because of Him." Her groans started up again.

"Don't be afraid," the donkey comforted her. "He won't take your baby. Not *our* He! I *know* He won't."

But the cow moaned.

"Listen to me," Manni urged. "I tell you I know Him well. You must trust Him. I've seen every creature that was knocked down in the forest with the thunder-stick. It was always for mercy. And I've told you there's never been a young one among them. Never! And He'll spare yours too."

An hour passed. As dawn was coming softly, Peter stepped into the barn. He had been expecting Lisa's calving for days and had been keeping close watch on her day and night. He had a bucket in his hands and a lighted lantern.

At sight of Lisa's crowded stall, he laughed. "Now, look, children, this is impossible. I need room so I can help her. Go away!" He patted the smooth shanks of the horses and added, "Go on. Be reasonable. There, boy—there, good girl—there."

Obediently the horses returned to their stalls.

The stallion whispered to Witch, "I'm really concerned about the baby."

"No reason to be," answered the mare, also in a whisper. "He only wants to help her."

"Manni, you're in my way," scolded Peter in a gentle voice.

"That Gray has to meddle in everything," the stallion muttered.

Peter went to work, relieving the cow's pain as best he could. Lisa felt the relief he brought her, and after another half hour Peter held the little calf in his arms.

He took several handfuls of bran from his bucket and sprinkled them over the small moist body. Then he carefully stood the calf on its unsteady legs near its mother. "There you are." He gave Lisa a friendly smile. "The rest is *your* affair."

The calf stood dizzily while Lisa proudly washed it with her tongue. Peter saw that everything was in order and that the calf was muzzling for its milk. He caressed the cow's flanks. "That was pretty well done," he said, and went out of the barn.

He was no sooner gone than the horses rushed to Lisa's stall.

"Oh, what a cute baby!" cried the mare.

"It's beautiful all right," the stallion admitted.

Manni asked Lisa, "Now you're happy, aren't you?"

The cow didn't answer, but went on washing her baby.

"Never forget the help that He gave you," said the donkey.

"He and His help! I don't trust it," whispered the stallion.

Lisa lifted her head and uttered a loud cry of despair. Her big dark eyes showed returning fear.

"*Must* you frighten her?" the donkey scolded Devil. "You ought to be grateful yourself and you talk like a base ingrate!"

"I'm only warning her, that's all," Devil defended himself. "Just in case—"

"Well, your warning isn't needed!" Manni grew angry. "He was good to the milk-giver. He's always good to us, always does the very best He can for us." He turned back to Lisa. "You'd better be grateful and stop being so suspicious! Nobody's going to take your baby!"

"I hope you're right," Lisa sighed. She resumed her washing.

"How that baby drinks!" Witch said gently.

"It tastes good to him," remarked Devil, who felt somewhat ashamed now.

Thoughtfully, contentedly, Manni watched the cow and her calf.

Chapter 7

THE THUNDER-STICK HAD SPOKEN
again.

Martin had known that it would, and
stayed home.

A dangerous outlaw stag had to be killed. He had run
amok. With his two sharp daggers he had threatened to
murder or wound every opponent he could find. He had
been attacking all the other stags—until Peter found him.

And now Arilla, the dead outlaw's mate, would not
move from beside his body.

Even when Peter lifted his victim up and carried him away, Arilla slipped along too, hidden in the thicket. She looked mournfully at the dangling head of her mate. When it finally disappeared from sight, she sent forth a trembling farewell.

"How beautiful he was! How wonderfully beautiful and proud!"

She wept, for she thought she was alone.

"Proud?" Rabot, a young buck, joined her. "Proud as evil!"

"No!" she contradicted him. "He was brave—the bravest of all!"

"With a crown like his it was easy to be brave."

Arilla broke into fresh tears. "That crown! Long, straight as a fir, and so richly pearled! With points as blindingly white as sapling wood when he had rubbed off their covering!"

"Those sharp points were deadly and he threatened everyone with them!"

"Yes." Arilla straightened up proudly. "You feared him. Everyone feared him."

"Does that seem good to you? That is certainly a worthy ambition to have! To make everyone afraid of you!"

"Well, it *is*." Arilla tossed her head. "Then you're respected. No one attacks you. No one dares to."

"You're wrong, Arilla. Listen, I'm your friend—we're all friends together, aren't we?"

"Ye-es."

"All right, then tell me: who was his friend? Not a single one of us!"

"He didn't need any friends!"

"Oh, now you're wrong again. Everybody needs friends. Having friends gives a fine feeling of security. Friends make life happy."

Arilla kept her head turned away. "He had a feeling of security. Because—"

"Because he fought so? Wait a minute. Wait a minute. He might have been secure against attack without so much violence. None of us ever thinks of attacking another one of us. We fight a little bit in mating time, yes. But apart from that we're always peaceful.

You think he was respected? Well, he wasn't. Fear isn't respect. When I'm afraid, I avoid the one who makes me afraid, but to my mind he was a bad fellow and I pay no respect to a bad fellow!" Rabot ended emphatically.

"He *wasn't* bad," Arilla protested; "not to me. He was good to me."

"Now you *are* mistaken!" Rabot retorted sharply. "You can hold it against me if you want to. But I say you're badly mistaken. Every one of us knows he was rude to you. Domineering and ill-tempered! A bully! Deny it if you can!"

Arilla dropped her head. "I can't," she whispered. "But I loved him. His death hurts me."

"That's something else again, Arilla. But you're alone in your love and your sorrow."

"You mean nobody liked him at all? Nobody is sorry he's dead?"

"No one! In fact everybody's pleased he's gone!"

Arilla shuddered. "How horrible!"

"Yes, it *is* horrible to have no friends to mourn you.

Now you see, Arilla, what it really means to be 'proud,' and 'brave,' and everything else that you say about him. He was a ruffian, a terror to all who wanted to live peacefully. An object of hatred! Now he's gone and we all feel relieved. So you must stop grieving. He was never worthy of your love and he's not worth your sorrow."

"Is this just your queer way of consoling me?" Arilla whispered in distressed suspicion.

"No! But it *should* console you—to learn the plain truth. If you don't believe *me*, wait and see whether anybody else has a bit of regret for him."

Arilla stood wretchedly. Then she broke out with, "I never thought—I never believed that He would do anything to him! That He would kill him with His thunder-stick—He, who was always so gentle!"

"And just. Gentle and just. Do you deny that He's just?"

"Yes! Yes! I do! I can never have confidence in Him again!"

A fawn came up to join in the talk. "Don't be bitter, Arilla. You forget how good He has always been to us."

A few others, bucks and fawns, arrived.

"We're all grateful for His generosity," a strong roe-buck said decisively.

Members of the group around him agreed loudly.

"That's right!"

"He deserves our confidence!"

"Yes, even our love–"

"Why, in the winter He sees to it that we don't starve!"

Arilla looked pleadingly around the circle. "But you aren't *all* glad He killed my mate–?"

A chorus of "Yes! Yes, we are!" answered her.

"He's given us peace from a murderer," a handsome buck declared.

"Just as we've hoped He would," added another. "We've all been hoping for this very thing. We expected it of Him. We trusted Him to come and help us. And now He's done it–He's put an end to the wretch."

The last speaker pushed forward. "Look, Arilla, look at me." He showed his flank along which ran a wide scar. "That's a little token your mate gave me. Only a miracle saved me then! I was sick and weak for a long time and suffered horrible pain!"

"Are you still surprised, Arilla?" Rabot asked quietly. "Or do you think we're cruel?"

She shook her head silently.

And then, all at once, they were saying: "We're sorry for you, Arilla! . . . We always pitied you. . . . You were blinded. . . . You can begin a new life now. . . . Yes, yes, a new life, no longer enslaved . . . no longer mistreated . . . no longer intimidated. . . . You'll learn of love . . . of tenderness, from another mate. . . ."

But Arilla would not listen anymore. She made a sudden leap and fled.

"Poor fool," was Rabot's judgment. Still, for a long time he gazed after her.

The buck with the scar concluded: "Well, anyway, we're rid of that tyrant. Now we can live without fear again."

Chapter 8

OFF AND ON FOR A LONG TIME Shah the Persian tomcat had been ranging the forest. Peter had tried hard to ambush him, but the cat had succeeded in outwitting his master. At length Peter laid a snare and caught him. Shah was now facing his last moment on earth, for the tender-hearted Peter had steeled himself to execute his pet for preying on the little forest folk.

But Shah sprang out of the box trap so gracefully and

innocently, and purred around Peter so lovingly, that he was not condemned, but pardoned instead. Martin and Babette welcomed the tomcat into the house again as if a beloved prodigal had returned, repentant.

Shah, however, did not know he had sinned and knew even less of repentance. So he accepted the welcoming caresses of his master as his just due. Condescendingly, in an offhand manner, he renewed his friendship with Treff, the hunting dog.

"Come on," Shah whispered. "I want to see the horses again and Gray and the cow."

"The cow's just had a calf."

"That's fine," Shah said casually.

Treff sniffed the tomcat. "You smell of the forest. You smell interesting."

"I had a nice time there," Shah admitted.

They stole out of the house and ran to the stable.

At sight of Shah, Manni exclaimed, "You back again?"

"We thought you'd died," Devil neighed.

Shah swaggered around the stallion's legs. "On the contrary, I lived richly and happily."

"Who fed you?" asked Witch naïvely.

Shah gave himself still greater airs. "No one! I fed myself. A pheasant one day, a hare the next. In between, sometimes a squirrel or a jay. I tell you, it was a wonderful life!"

"Murder," grumbled Lisa, "murder . . ."

Shah arched his back and challenged the cow. "I dare you to say that again!"

"Don't listen to her," Devil soothed him. "She's stupid."

"I can't understand what's so wonderful about killing other creatures," Manni put in. "But since I don't understand it I won't express an opinion."

"No," Witch agreed, "I won't give my opinion about it either."

Devil shook his mane. "Such things are strange to us."

"Right!" chuckled the Persian; "you're soft grass-eaters. But *this* one's my friend." Shah rubbed tenderly along Treff's flank. "He understands me. He envies me!"

"Maybe I do," Treff admitted. "I can imagine how

happy you were. But I could never do anything like that myself. I have too much conscience."

"Never mind." Shah's manner was condescending. "You're a good fellow. Even if we are different, we can still be friends, can't we?"

For answer Treff wagged his tail and pushed the cat over onto his back. He playfully seized Shah's throat in his jaws while Shah braced both hind paws against the dog's shaggy chest.

"Aren't you afraid?" called Witch.

Lithely the Persian sprang up. "Of course not!"

"What if he should bite you?" the stallion asked worriedly.

Shah was amused. "He doesn't bite hard. Any more than I ever hurt him with my claws."

Treff chuckled too.

"Are you going to stay with us now?" Manni inquired of the tomcat.

"I feel like staying," Shah admitted. "It's very comfortable here with Him. I don't have to exert myself. There's plenty of milk, which I'll confess I missed up there. And there's also a warm little corner where I can sleep without being disturbed."

Witch looked puzzled. "How can you be in the forest alone so long without a master, and now be so nicely obedient again?"

"Obedient?" Shah was surprised. "I don't know what it is to be obedient. And don't call Him my master. I know no master. He's my friend." Shah stretched and yawned. "I wanted to see Him again. I'm quite fond of Him. Just the same, He didn't have to catch me in a wooden box! That wasn't a friendly thing to do. But I suppose He thought it was the only way. That was it—He put it there because he longed for me! Touching, isn't it? During that night in the box I hoped He'd come quickly. I wanted to see Him too. And the forest—well, I wasn't really having any fun in the forest anymore. So now I'm going to stay here."

Manni looked skeptically at the tomcat. After a short silence he said: "But suppose you should *want* to go again?"

Shah was washing himself. He paused and admitted

casually: "Of course, if I *want* to, naturally I'll go. But not to stay so long again. Only for a night. For a pheasant," he added. "It's as good as caught. They sleep in the trees, and sleep quite soundly. No, I won't need to stay any longer than one night another time."

"What about Him?" asked Devil. "Will He stand for it?"

"He won't find out anything! He's far from being as smart as I am."

"Oh, go on with you!" Manni snickered. "You really mean you think you're smarter than He is?"

"I certainly do and I certainly am," Shah said as if stating obvious facts.

Even Treff looked unconvinced.

Amiably the Persian explained to him: "You know I always do only what I want to do. Unlike you, I serve no one. I follow only my own will. For instance, right *now*—I've had enough of all of you." He squeezed through the barn's swinging door, and Treff pushed through after him.

"Stuck-up thing!" the stallion neighed indignantly.

Chapter 9

CLOSE BY, MARTIN COULD HEAR the finch singing his gay little song, fresh and sprightly as a short poem in lilting rhythm. Over and over he repeated the melody, for he knew no other. Between spurts of music he flashed his quick *Psst! Psst!* as if calling someone's attention. Then he started his sweet little song anew.

Martin was sitting on his observation platform in the treetops, close to the edge of a small clearing in an out-of-the-way part of the preserve. He had a lovely view from here of branch and foliage, and the little meadow and its grass and bog.

Again the song of the finch sounded. Nearby three other finches sang happily to one another. The first finch joined them.

Under Martin's very nose, on the railing of the observation platform, sat a forest mouse, staring as if spellbound. When the young man moved a trifle, she jumped a little distance away, then paused for an instant as if to make up her mind. She threw him one more glance and disappeared as if by magic.

A little squirrel leaped onto the railing. He stopped in amazement as if saying, "Oh, look!" Then he made a flying leap right over Martin to the trunk of a tree.

Beneath Martin suddenly something rushed close to the ground—a burst of sparkling color. It was the kingfisher flashing by, and again Martin's desire to see him at close range was aroused. But in vain. Martin had never seen him except by lucky circumstance. He had caught a glimpse of him once, hardly bigger than a child's fist, earnestly balancing on a branch with his very short legs. The kingfisher was never to be seen walking or hopping; only in swift flight or, once in a great while, sitting very still.

A fluttering above him took Martin's mind from the unattainable. A crow, obviously trying to escape an enemy, came through the trees on frightened wings.

The enemy she could have killed with a single stroke of her strong bill was a tiny golden oriole. But she fled from him madly as he flew under her, hacking furiously at her belly, giving up only when she escaped into open space. Then he flew back, still indignant, returning to the nest where he had surprised the robber crow about to murder and eat his brood.

Martin was reminded by this dramatic scene that the sense of property and parenthood can lift the weakest to genuine courage, and that the strong are made cowardly and defenseless by the feeling of guilt.

The stately hare, serious as always, sat quietly on the edge of the clearing, unable to reach a decision of any kind. He bent his ears forward, then pressed them flat against his back. His white whiskers trembled with his incessant scenting of the air. He looked up with tilted head, the very picture of a father distracted by anxiety.

Completely unworried, a roe strolled about. Unlike the hare, he did not scent the breeze or jerk his head up. He merely nibbled, daintily moving his thin legs.

The hoopoe, raising his semicircular crest mistrustfully, eyed the roe with curiosity, half wanting to go closer to him, half shunning acquaintance. After a moment he made off into the thicket.

Far below, the flight of water wagtails entranced Martin—a flight without wide curves. And he was amused by their pretty walk, in which they nodded agreeably to one another, both with their little heads and their narrow tails, as if to express how good the world seemed to them.

Suddenly Tambo appeared.

The roe did not notice him at first. When he did he leaped away without emitting a sound of fright. But after a few moments, from a distance, Martin heard twice his *Ba-uh!*

Only the hare remained in his place. He was not afraid of Tambo.

Magnificent and proud, yet somehow timidly embarrassed, Tambo stood in full view. Martin saw that the stag paused to watch the roe's flight. Tambo remained motionless a minute, then majestically yet swiftly vanished into the underbrush.

Now, three, four, five king pheasants walked regally across the clearing. Streaks of radiant gold and black gleamed on their bodies like ceremonial vestments, and ceremoniously they dragged behind them the long train of their tailfeathers. Their passage, Martin thought, was like a procession of archbishops.

When the sun was high in the heavens and silence fell in the forest, Martin went home reflecting:

"We always remain strange to them. They don't understand us. They don't know what an endless measure of inspiration they are, what a font of mystery and magic. No. We fill them only with fear and enmity. It's been in their blood since the oldest times, and has become their sharpest instinct. It is sad. And the worst of it is that I suppose we human beings are responsible for it."

Chapter 10

ISA THE COW CRIED OUT AT HEAR-
ing human footsteps approaching. Her terror was so great this time that her stable
companions were alarmed and confused.

"They're coming!" she cried, whipping her flanks
with her tail. "They'll take my baby from me!" She
pressed the calf into a far corner of her stall. It stood
there close under the crib trembling and bawling miserably.

The horses stretched their necks over the wall.

"Be still, mother," whispered Witch. "How often have we told you nothing will happen to your baby?"

Devil contradicted Witch with a snort. "You're right, mother. You can never tell what He will do."

Manni turned to Devil. "That's just like you! Why do you tease the good soul?"

To annoy Manni the stallion neighed, "Defend yourself, mother! Defend yourself!"

When Martin and Peter entered the stable, the cow had her head lowered, ready to gore wildly. But both men passed her by and went to the horses instead.

"Well, which one shall I saddle?" Peter asked.

"The mare," Martin decided. He glanced at Lisa who was glaring and kept switching her tail. "Odd how the cow's behaving."

Peter, putting the bit on the mare, looked over at the cow. "She does seem a little excited." He strapped the saddle firmly on Witch.

Lisa became somewhat more quiet.

Martin put a foot in the stirrup, swung onto Witch's back and guided her out. Peter stayed behind and went over to the cow. He petted her between the horns and offered her a handful of salt. "Well, how's your calf, Lisa?"

His gentle tone soothed Lisa. Hesitantly at first, then more confidently, she licked the salt from his hand. His other hand caressed her thick brown neck.

Babette's voice was heard suddenly. "I want to see how the calf's getting on."

At once Lisa began to lash her tail again.

"That calf will be very beautiful," Babette said. She would have entered the stall but Lisa blocked the way and snorted wildly.

"Don't come in!" Peter said. "She doesn't want you to."

"If you don't"–Babette smiled at Lisa–"then I won't."

She and Peter left the stable.

The stallion was triumphant. "You're very brave. You chased them away, mother!"

"Yes, they're gone," Lisa mooed softly. "My baby wasn't touched."

The donkey brayed his kindly but incredulous laughter.

Chapter 11

GRAY CLOUDS COVERED THE BLUE skies. The fall had lost its patience and would be delayed no longer by the lingering summer. It broke forth with furor.

Cold wind swept foliage from the trees. Cold rain splashed down and countless leaves fell, so that many trees were suddenly left with bare limbs.

A radiant morning followed. Its cool freshness made the forest look new born. The air was crisp and sparkling. In the meadows and clearings mellow frost lay like sprinkled sugar. This glittering cover did not melt until the sun mounted high. Then wilted grass appeared.

O-eh! came the first bay of a stag.

Soon a second and third rang through the woods.

Fascinated, Martin listened to this primitive sound which came only at one time of the year. By tomorrow the forest would be filled with the mighty trumpeting of the stags.

With the first pink of dawn Martin went stalking, accompanied by Peter. Peter carried a gun hung on his shoulder, for he was prepared—just in case. But Martin, as always, had no weapon. Worshiping every living creature, he could not bear to kill.

When they reached the forest, Peter turned off and Martin went on alone. He breathed deeply of the sharp air and watched his warm breath vanish like thin smoke.

The roaring of the stags sounded. Martin stood stock-still to listen. With his finely tuned senses, he could tell the voices apart. Now one bayed. And then another cry thundered deep and throaty.

The voices of the younger animals pealed clearly. In

contrast sounded the commanding basses of the Kings.

Martin walked the narrow trail step by step, carefully avoiding every dry twig that might crack. But suddenly close to him came a rustling and breaking. A stag rushed by, so near that Martin could have touched him. Martin groped his way on noiselessly.

About eighty paces ahead in the bush, something dark moved. Then came a mighty roaring.

That was he–Martin's favorite, monarch of the forest. It was from him that the other had fled.

Tambo bayed forth. His black mane stretched almost horizontally, so that his brown crown seemed to lie on his back. The roaring came from the depth of his breast. Martin could see its power, a cloud of steam floating in the morning air.

A number of stately does, seven in all, huddled together close to Tambo, their ears moving. They were rapt in awe of their tyrant husband.

Completely hidden in the thicket an older, weaker stag lurked in ambush, waiting to see whether in a lucky moment he could steal one of the seven, but at the same time ready for flight.

The does listened to Tambo, faithfully admiring him, but at the same time prepared to desert him should another woo them.

When one started to slip off into the bush, Tambo leaped over and drove the fugitive back to her place with a few admonishing blows with his antlers. She accepted the punishment without protest.

Tambo bayed in triumph.

Deep and continuous in the near distance sounded the baying of an old stag. It rose in a clearer, higher sound, fell off and began again at once. This new voice drowned out all others. It was a challenge to a struggle, a mockery of the weak and cowardly, and a proud woo- ing. Tambo cocked his head to listen.

That, Martin realized, must be the giant King who, a few years before, had carried fourteen points, but had recently reverted to ten. Now his big crown ended in long, blank spears which shone like ivory.

His baying grew closer. The other stags were silent, frightened and tense. Tambo waited as the great voice came.

Martin felt anxious. In spite of his aversion for killing,

he almost hoped that Peter was at hand, to shoot the old warrior in Tambo's defense if necessary.

And then the old stag appeared at the edge of the thicket. He stood motionless for a second, before he plunged berserk at Tambo.

Tambo seemed about to sacrifice himself, so close did he let the old one come. With swift agility, he executed a slight turn and lowered his crown a bit.

Dully the two heads crashed. At once, with a somewhat sharper sound, the antlers knocked together.

Each fighter strained against the other, snorting, putting forth his entire strength. Their eyes were bloodshot. They breathed in short gasps. The old stag jumped backward.

As the pressure against him withdrew suddenly, Tambo stumbled forward. This, the watching Martin knew, was the moment of greatest danger.

But before the old one could drive his horns into Tambo's exposed flank, a shot rang out!

Martin saw the mighty stag leap into the air once and again; saw his eyes open wide with amazement; saw his convulsive staggering; saw death force down into the wilted meadow grass a great animal that just now had been full of life.

The does had disappeared. Tambo too had vanished.

Martin, shaken and trembling, met Peter by the old stag's body, looked down into the dead eyes which shimmered glassy green. He heard Peter mutter, "I didn't want to shoot you down, old fellow, but I had to."

Martin sighed. "That's how it always is! Age dies that youth may live."

"Don't feel too badly about him," said Peter. "His end came at a moment of victory. And it was sudden. Better than if he'd had to die slowly, like other senile animals. He'd have been dethroned, and wandered around humiliated. He'd have died gradually with great suffering. Now he's been spared that."

Yet his mood of depression continued as Martin wandered home.

Chapter 12

JUST BEFORE DAWN ONE LATE FALL morning the roe Genina, with her two kids, came to the Forest Lodge. They stepped gingerly around the house, where the human beings were still sleeping. Treff pricked up his ears, but did not bark.

The roes wandered toward the stable where the doors opened at the slightest touch. Followed by both her young, Genina stepped into the warm space which was filled with the odor of sleeping animals.

"It's pleasant here," said Genina to her children. "Let's stay. We'll be safe."

Manni stood up quickly at the sound and stared in amazement at the intruders. "Look! Look!" he cried to his sleeping companions. "The wild ones from the forest!" He went toward Genina, still unbelieving. "Why did you leave the forest? Anything wrong there?"

The others awoke, and all marveled over the guests. They stared at them curiously, but welcomed them, glad they had come.

Witch inquired, "Poor things, haven't you anything to eat?"

"Oh, we have enough," Genina answered. "Sweet hay, chestnuts and turnips. Yes, we're full."

"What's the matter then?" asked Manni. "No thunder-stick is crashing now."

"I know. It is not your He that we are so afraid of. If we were, we wouldn't have come here."

"Whom are you afraid of?" demanded the stallion.

"There are others—who murder without the thunder-stick."

"How?" Manni wanted to know. "No He can kill without a thunder-stick."

"That's what you think," the roe mother retorted. "I don't understand how, myself, but they murder us much more cruelly than with the thunder-stick. You hear nothing, see nothing. Suddenly you can't move from the spot. You writhe helplessly, gasping for air. But no use! Life is over only after great torture."

"Oh, come on! That's hard to believe!" snorted Devil.

"Just the same, it's true," sighed the roe. "Many hares have fallen victim to this strange death, a few grownups of my family, five or six of our young. And when you have two little ones . . ."

"Nothing will happen to you here with us," Lisa consoled the roe. The cow had forgotten now that she had ever been afraid of her two-legged guardians herself.

"I hope not," Genina sighed; "but you really don't know anymore whom you can trust."

"You can trust us completely," Witch affirmed.

"And our two-legged ones as well," Manni nodded.

"Yes, I know them," said the roe mother. "They do no evil."

The kids, Mena and Loso, had hung timidly behind their mother.

"Here you are, little ones. Have some." Devil pushed his crib a little so that some oats fell to the floor. The twins scrambled for the grain, seeking it out gaily and eagerly in the straw, treating themselves to the new and strange meal.

"You're quite different from us," Genina said suddenly.

"Obviously." The stallion drew himself up very tall. "You can see that from the size of our bodies."

"As far as that goes," the roe said, "we have distinguished relatives in the forest who are no smaller than you. And besides, they wear wonderful crowns."

The surprise of the horses, the cow and the calf, amused the mother roe. Manni of course recalled seeing Tambo. The doe continued: "What I meant was that your way of life is different from ours."

"Decidedly," Devil agreed. "We don't live such dangerous lives."

"We live much more comfortably than you do," cried Manni.

"Our life is simply grand!" Witch spoke enthusi-
astically.

"Yes, I see. But I wouldn't change with you for anything," Genina remarked.

"Yet you've come here to us," snorted the stallion.

"Yes, because I had to. I was afraid for my little ones.
Otherwise I wouldn't be here with you."

Manni was curious. "Why not? Why wouldn't you
like to lead our beautiful kind of life?"

"Because you lack the most precious thing of all."

"To be knocked over by the thunder-stick or to be
tortured to death?" mocked the stallion.

"You don't understand. I mean our freedom. Even
the thunder-stick—it's hurled very rarely after all—and
even slow death by torture belong with our good life.
Our wonderful freedom isn't destroyed so easily. Freedom can never be paid for too dearly!" The mother roe
stood radiant in her grace and pride.

The animals of the stable were all silent, bewildered
but moved by an unconscious respect for the delicate
little creature.

The stallion as usual lost patience first. "Describe this freedom to us."

"I can't. To know it and understand it, you must live in freedom from your first day on earth."

Devil pawed impatiently. "Why?"

"None of you can possibly understand. You're His servants. You're fond of Him and you obey Him. That's the difference between you and us. That's what really makes us strangers to one another."

"Strangers!" Witch echoed. "I think we're getting along together very well indeed."

"Of course we are. And I think I could be quite devoted to all of you. But—but there's a deep gulf between us just the same. You don't envy me my way of life and I envy you yours even less. . . . Oh, let's not talk about it anymore." She made herself comfortable, closed her eyes and was asleep almost immediately. The two kids slept nearby, exhausted by the excitement of their new adventure.

Witch bent down and breathed over Genina. "Isn't she pretty?"

"A little sure of herself, it seems to me," Devil puffed.

"Not at all," Manni defended Genina. "She's an innocent, simple thing."

Lisa looked over. "The two little ones are adorable."

Now there was deep silence. The horses, the donkey, Lisa and the calf dozed off too. They were all waiting to be fed and watered. Lisa longed to be milked.

It was almost daylight when Babette entered the stable. Peter came in right behind her. At their heavy steps, the roes leaped up frightened, and fled into the farthest corner where the kids huddled close to their mother.

"Look! Peter, look!" cried Babette. "Roes! From the forest! Oh, how beautiful!" she whispered. She went over to them and caressed one after the other. They trembled under her hand. "Don't be afraid," she murmured softly. "I won't hurt you. Peter, why do you suppose they've come to us?"

"It's almost a miracle," Peter answered.

He and Babette hurried to the house to tell Martin about the surprising visitors.

Manni mused, "Wouldn't it be fine if He understood our speech, and we didn't have to guess at His!"

"We can guess only vaguely what He says and means," grumbled the stallion.

Manni whispered to the roes, "If such understanding were possible, you could tell Him what goes on in the forest."

"Yes, but it's a vain hope," sighed Witch.

"A vain hope," repeated the mother roe. "I never think of hoping anything like that. It makes me tremble to have Him come so close to me, to have Him touch me. Somehow even though I know He will do us no harm, He makes me terribly afraid—and my little ones too."

"But that's foolish." Manni tried to calm her. "He's so good and kind."

"Don't be afraid, youngsters," Witch said to the twins.

Meanwhile Martin was hearing about the new arrivals. He was amazed. "Why would roes come to the barn?"

"In flight," Peter suggested.

"But from whom? From what?"

"I'm sure they were chased here by something," Babette said. "Maybe a fox."

"Come on, I must see them," said Martin and they all went back to the animals. While Babette busied herself milking Lisa, and Peter fed and watered the others, Martin stood by the roes. He was too puzzled to caress or touch them.

"Give them clover," he said, "and some oats."

In the corner where the roes had fled Peter made a bed for them. He piled clover before them and liberally poured out oats.

"I don't understand this at all," Martin said in bewilderment.

"Now that I think about it, it isn't so hard to figure," muttered Peter. "Poachers! They might be at it pretty badly!"

"Yes, that might be it," Martin said and his face flushed with sudden anger.

"Might be? I'm sure of it! A roe doesn't run here with her kids for nothing."

"But I heard no shooting."

"You're—well, sir, may I say innocent? They're mighty careful to make no noise. They lay out traps, the scoundrels!"

"Peter, we've got to put a stop to it."

The older man said nothing. He only nodded grimly.

Chapter 13

PETER WAS SCOUTING THROUGH the forest, staying on the trails when he thought he might be seen by any other human being at large in the preserve, breaking through thickets to stalk along wild paths when he could be neither seen nor heard.

For a long time he found nothing. Then a squadron of crows gathered somewhere close by in the brush, cawing and flapping their wings.

Peter turned toward where the sound came from.

At his approach the crows flew off, leaving behind the remains of a deer. This, Peter could tell, was where the poachers had cut up the prey. But where had the roe been killed? Peter's expert eyes made out a man's footprints, alternately deep and shallow in the soft ground.

He followed them. Now he could see marks in the drying grass where the garrotted roe had been dragged along.

So the criminal had not cut and divided the body where he had snared his victim. "A cunning fellow!" thought Peter in disgust.

It was easy to follow the trail; fur caught here and there on the branches of low bushes showed the way. Peter came to a crossing of two wide paths made by stags and does. Peter knew, for trails made by hares and other small animals are thin as threads.

"And," he thought to himself, "that fellow knows too." He came to a spot where the earth had been dug up and the bushes trampled down—the spot on which the roe's death struggle had been played out.

Peter had learned enough for one day. He went

home by a roundabout route. "Scoundrels are at work, that's sure," he muttered. "But—one, or two?"

When he told Martin what he had discovered rage drove color into the hunchback's face. He whispered hoarsely, "I'll help you find out!"

Peter objected. "I'd rather you didn't do anything, sir—take your usual walk, follow your regular trails. That'll be less likely to cause suspicion."

"But I want to—"

Peter broke in. "You understand, sir, that catching the fellow now is the most difficult thing. Only one of us can do it. Leave everything to me, won't you, please?"

Martin looked helplessly into Peter's determined face. But he knew Peter was right, and thereafter the older man continued his stalking expeditions day after day alone.

For days he found nothing—no snares, no traps. Every evening Martin asked for results, but Peter only shook his head.

He had seen more than enough in the way of evidence: the roe's remains, the dragging trail, the prints of boots, the place on the roe trail where the trapped animal jerked itself to death. Proof upon proof of evil. But he could not find the evil-doer.

Then, after two days more of wasted time, Peter found a snare in the midst of a thicket. It hung barely a hand's breadth above the ground.

"This is for a hare," he said to himself.

With the utmost care he avoided leaving any trace of his own presence. But here and there he broke a thin twig so that it swung loosely. He marked the way by sticking a dry branch with a few wilted leaves into the ground in an inconspicuous spot.

He decided this was the place to watch if he were going to surprise the poacher. But he mustn't come too close, or he might defeat his own purpose. As long as no hare dangled in the snare the poacher would not crawl into the bush. If caught outside, he could say he had only been taking a walk, although walking here in the preserve was prohibited to strangers.

Another two days Peter visited the snare, but with no results. On the third day he observed a quaking of the bushes around the snare. A hare must have been caught and was struggling to free himself.

"Poor little fellow," he thought, "how gladly I'd help you! But I can't. You must die so that the lives of many other creatures may be saved."

He tested his flashlight, loaded one barrel of his shotgun with buckshot and crawled close to the snare.

The hare was struggling wildly, violently, with desperate leaps into the air which only trussed him tighter. Finally his efforts grew weaker and weaker.

"Shameful torture," thought Peter, who was himself suffering with the trapped creature.

With the coming of twilight the hare was still. "It's all over, poor fellow," thought Peter.

The twilight slid into night and soon the half-moon shone palely from the sky.

Stealthily someone moved nearby. Almost with admiration Peter noted how cleverly the fellow slithered through the thicket. Now he must be with his victim. . . . Now he would have his booty. . . . Now he was getting away!

Peter leaped out to bar his path, snapping on his flashlight. The man gave a cry.

"Stop!" Peter gasped, breathless with anger.

He saw the hare fall from the poacher's hands.

"Stop or I'll shoot!" Peter swung the gun barrel lower. "Not a step!" he warned.

With difficulty he repressed his rage. Now that he had caught the miscreant, he wanted to deal with him coolly. He ordered: "Pick up the hare."

The fellow obeyed fumblingly.

Peter threw the flashlight beam into his face.

The man was in his middle years, pale as a corpse, the picture of cringing fear. He fell to his knees. "Have mercy! This is the first time I've—"

Peter kicked at him scornfully. "Get up!" After taking the hare, he tied the man's hands. "Now get along!"

The man whined. "Don't lead me like this, tied up like a criminal!"

"You're worse than a criminal! Move on!" Peter jabbed the shotgun barrel into the small of the fellow's back.

Reaching the Forest Lodge with his captive, he reported: "Caught in the act!"

Martin and Babette, silent and shocked, looked at the strangled hare and at the prisoner.

"I'm taking him to the police," Peter declared.

The poacher let out a cry and looked appealingly to Martin. But the little humpback, staring at the dead hare, shook his head and turned away.

Chapter 14

THE DEER JOINED TOGETHER AND moved about in herds. Forgotten now was every battle—all competition, envy, anger, humiliating defeat or proud victory. For the time of mating, so recently over, no longer lived in the memory of the stags.

Peace came again to those with the high crowns. The gentleness of their natures asserted itself. They bedded down close together; they marched through the forest and appeared together at the feeding places. They did not quarrel.

Now there was no difference between the strong and the weak; only a willing recognition of the elder by the younger.

The youngest and the weakest moved in the lead. Behind them came the stags of middle strength, and finally the very strong. This was not a matter of rank, but a mysterious age-old measure of strategy by which the weak were sacrificed to protect the ablest.

Now in winter they still had their crowns. Tambo, though he showed only twelve points, paced along at the rear, while others, ahead, carried crowns with fourteen, even sixteen points. Yet this order was fair, for Tambo was obviously superior, not only by the might of his horns, but by the power of his body. No other stag could compare with him.

Most of the birds had long since fallen mute. Many had sought southern lands where there was neither snow nor cold, where sunshine always gave warmth and nourishment.

The blackbirds, ill-humored and with ruffled feathers, crouched hardly visible on tree branches, or hacked at snow-free spots on the ground for something, anything, to eat.

The pheasants sat still on their sleeping-trees. After awaking late they swung down to the ground and let out a cackling, more muted than usual and sounding like a poor attempt to crow. They minced to places under the house eaves where He had strewn buckwheat for them. Only the magpies chattered now and then, not so talkative as usual, but never quite silent.

The many crows cawed loudly as they flew eagerly about, spying about for dead and dying forest residents. Screeching, they gathered around some victim to gobble their meal while they quarreled noisily.

Completely silent, commanding in their dignity, the stags proceeded through the forest. They paid no attention at all to the does, just as if there had never been ardent wooing or fierce fighting over them.

A few paces behind Tambo, Debina followed the stags. This young doe constantly kept close to the crown-bearers, standing modestly beside them in the hay fields where clover, chestnuts and burgundy turnips grew enticingly. The stags endured Debina's presence as if she weren't there.

A day came when Tambo felt that itching on his head which he dimly recalled from previous years. His twelve-pointed crown began to feel heavy—strange and lifeless as if it did not belong to him at all. He grew nervous. Deliberately he hit the crown against strong branches. It withstood the shock. Nevertheless his nervousness increased. He felt feverish and queerly impatient.

He did not bump his crown against a tree again, but suddenly, after days and days, its roots dissolved in a few minutes and it tumbled down into the snow.

With a quick feeling of freedom Tambo lifted his head. From the pores of the two smooth, iron-colored plates on which the crown had rested, tiny drops of blood seeped out.

But Tambo knew nothing of that. He felt no pain. Presently, though, the frosty air blew across both plates and made him realize his baldness. Humiliating shame raged within him. At once he left the herd. He wandered lonely from now on, wanting to hide and not be seen by anyone.

But Debina remained on his trail tirelessly.

Still Tambo ignored her until she followed him into the thickest underbrush. He faced her suddenly. "What do you want?"

Debina hesitated, embarrassed, and said softly, "Nothing..."

"Why are you always around me?"

She dropped her young and beautiful head. "I don't know."

"Then go away. I want to be alone."

She looked into his eyes. "Let me do as I've been doing. I won't disturb you."

In a whisper, Tambo asked, "Did you belong to one of us? To me?"

"Oh, no!" She shuddered. "I was still too young. I escaped..."

"You won't find love anywhere now," he said gently.

Debina shook her head. "It's not that kind of love I want."

A little touched, he said, "Now I'm not crowned anymore. I'm just like all the others."

Timidly Debina took a tiny step toward him.

"You're not like the others. You are—" She paused. "It makes me happy just to see you—to be with you."

Tambo, falling mute, turned away and stepped very slowly through the leafless thicket. Just as slowly she followed him. They did not talk to each other. But Debina followed her chosen one, humbly, silently, faithfully, that day and for many days.

Tambo found himself growing strangely used to her. He became restless when he could not see her. And this time his period of baldness seemed less bothersome. Still his comradeship with Debina showed only in her constant presence, and in no other way at all.

Chapter 15

S PRING APPROACHED, MILD AND gentle, without down-pouring rain or storm. Occasional light clouds floated in the sky, then again its dome arched flawless, the palest greenish blue.

"Soon the loveliest season of all will be here," said Babette as she stood in the garden beside Martin.

"Spring comes to us like a healthy child, gay and smiling," Martin replied. He was holding a chestnut-leaf bud between his fingers and examining it. It had a coarse brown hull and was bursting with sap.

Genina, the mother roe, bounded about in front of the barn with her youngsters, Mena and Loso. In only a little while they would be almost fully grown.

Manni, frisking, joined them, for he was their devoted friend and playmate. Witch and Devil ambled sedately to and fro. Whenever they approached, the young roes fled.

"Still shy," grumbled Devil.

"They're afraid of you," Witch said.

"Why?"

"You know very well. Gray told you. They're frightened because you get such angry fits."

"Boring things!"

"No, they're good, gentle creatures."

Devil was jealous. "Just look—they go up to the cow and the calf without fear."

"They're relatives and the fat mother is so placid. She doesn't scare them as you do."

The stallion said bitterly, "Except for *me*, they seem to like their life here."

"Yes, they've adapted themselves wonderfully. Do you know, I–" Witch hesitated.

"You what?"

"Maybe I'm wrong, of course–but I really think it's true. I think those two young ones like their good safe life with us better than the horrid freedom their mother considers so precious."

Devil stared at the frolicking twins. "I believe you're right!" He stamped. "But why shouldn't they? What sensible creature wouldn't? What could be better than safety and plenty to eat without having to fight for it?"

"Of course I agree with you," Witch nodded.

The air was still sharp with the breath of snow, yet the roe family no longer slept in the stall. Mena and Loso wanted to, but their mother drove them outside, insisting that they sleep in the garden thicket by day and stay awake at night. When they protested shrilly, the mild Genina grew almost angry with her offspring. The animals who lived in the stable noticed that she wore an increasingly worried look.

Up in the forest, Genina knew, there had been no

trace of snow for several weeks, though its breath still came from the distant mountains. A fine light-green veil overspread the trees and bushes in the garden as she watched the young leaves announce their opening.

In the grass beside the wilting snowdrops, primroses bloomed. Here and there, tightly hugging the earth, a violet spread its fragrance. And the earth breathed a strong promise which filled all its wild creatures with hope and expectancy.

Morning and night on the highest treetops the blackbirds sang—short trial flights of their full summer melody.

With a strange abstraction the mother roe listened to these familiar fragments of music.

One evening near twilight she called her two children and led them hurriedly into the barn. Well-behaved, Mena and Loso stood behind their mother while she delivered a little speech to the stable animals.

"We're going home now," she told them softly. "Back to the forest—to freedom. Farewell to you all! And thank you. You've been very good to us—you and He—and we'll never forget it. But it's time now to take our leave. Come, little ones."

The animals clustered around, talking all at once.

"Stay a while longer, at least," Manni begged.

"You'll be sorry when you're back there fleeing from danger," said Lisa.

"Why must you ever leave at all?" Witch pleaded.

The mother roe was silent, looking at her youngsters.

"Oh, mother, we don't want to go!" Mena wept.

"It's much better here—we're warm and comfortable," declared Loso. "We get fed and cared for."

"Maybe it would have been better," Genina said in a low voice, "if we had stayed in the forest." Then quickly she put an end to conversation. "Farewell, friends! Come, you two!" She turned and ran out of the barn into the dusk, the twins reluctantly at her heels.

Devil shook his mane. "We'll never see them again."

"It's a great pity," Manni observed. "I liked those graceful three."

"I hope nothing evil happens to them," Witch sighed.

"Don't worry," Lisa raised her booming voice. "Whatever happens is fate and they chose it themselves."

Devil threw his head up high, yet kept still. Witch sighed again.

The calf too blew a sigh. "I'm sorry for them. Poor Mena and Loso—having to go back. But I envy them too."

"What a silly idea," Lisa said. The others stared at the calf, uncomprehending.

Meanwhile the three roes were slowly climbing uphill. They set their thin legs precisely one before the other. When they reached the forest they paused, their ears playing incessantly, their noses scenting the air eagerly.

"Here's our home," said the mother roe, moved; "the forest where you were born."

"Do you remember exactly where it was?" asked one of the youngsters.

"Certainly, Mena, my daughter."

"Take us there, mother!" demanded the other.

"That's exactly where I'm taking you, Loso."

And they pressed deeper into the forest. Genina soon found the trail the roes usually trod, closed in among bushes on which the young shoots bloomed invitingly, roofed over by high trees.

Mena called, "Why, it's beautiful here!"

"Isn't it!" said Genina with satisfaction.

"I remember–" Loso began softly.

"Really?" Genina was surprised. "That seems hardly possible, my son."

Still softer, Loso whispered: "I *think* I remember . . ."

"It only seems so to you."

Mena admitted, "I remember nothing. Everything is new and wonderful to me!"

"Yes!" Loso repeated, still whispering. "I *do* remember! I'm seeing pictures. They're hazy, but I know I've seen them before. I feel I've been here before."

"Well, my children," said Genina, her heart beating in violent excitement at being again in the forest, "you're both experiencing something good. To you, it's new, but it will soon be familiar to you, for we are home again." She was so moved she could not continue.

"And you, mother?" Mena crowded to her side. "How do you feel about it?"

Genina did not answer.

"You, mother"—Loso rubbed his forehead on her flank—"you have our feelings—and your own too."

A crackling and shaking from above them saved Genina the need for answer. Perri climbed down, waving her pert flag and jumping up and down with curiosity. "And who may you be?" she cried.

Genina sniffed at her. "Don't you know me anymore, Perri?"

"What? Genina? You alive?" Perri leaned back against her bushy tail, her eyes amazed.

"You can see I'm alive. My young ones too."

"I'm so glad!" The squirrel pressed her forepaw to her breast. "Everybody will be glad! We thought you'd suffered the choking torture death—you and your children. So many died miserably that way."

"That's why we went away."

Perri rushed up the tree. "I must tell everybody you're alive!" And she vanished.

Silently Genina and her children walked along the winding trail.

Eppi the weasel fled by, as fast as a red tongue of flame licking along the ground. Mena leaped into the air.

"You!" she cried. "I want to take a look at you!"

"Let Eppi alone," Genina chided her. "He's a robber."

Mena was surprised. "So small, and still a thief?"

"Yes, and a bloodthirsty one."

"Is there such a thing in the forest?" Loso asked innocently.

"There are many more besides Eppi," the mother warned. "Big murderers, too. We must be careful."

She turned off the path, slipped into the underbrush to reach a tiny hollow. "This is where it was, children! This is where you were born."

"Oh!" said Loso and Mena together. They looked around the narrow space fenced in by branches and believed they ought to feel something. But they felt nothing in particular.

Genina, on the other hand, was deeply touched. She lowered her head and stared at the ground.

She was remembering—remembering those far-off, painful, happy, busy hours. Fighting down her excitement, she turned to the silent Loso, to the mute Mena.

"Come on—let's go!"

Legs delicately lifting, she led the way back to the path. Relieved, the youngsters followed her. Not a single word was spoken. Presently a second trail united with the main one on which they were walking.

A stately roebuck was pulling and nibbling at the sprouting leaves of a hazel bush. His crown, though not yet fully developed, towered high and thickly covered.

Genina recognized him immediately. "Rombo!"

He paid no attention and did not move from where he was.

"Greetings, my Rombo!" called Genina. "Don't you recognize me?"

"Certainly," he said in a brief, distant tone.

"But you're so indifferent—" Genina hesitated, a foreleg in the air. "It's *I*! Genina! These are your children!"

"Better say *your* children," was the annoyed retort.

"Our children—" She stammered in confusion.

His head thrown high, Rombo said haughtily, "You didn't care what happened to me."

"Oh, I *did*. But–"

Carelessly he concluded, "I can't bother with you now–with any of you."

He disappeared into the thicket. Genina heard only the rustling of branches bent aside by his passage. Ashamed, she sniffed after him, inhaling his familiar odor. Puzzled like their mother, Loso and Mena sniffed too.

Finally Loso took courage. "Was that our father?"

Mena wanted an explanation. "Is he angry at us?"

"No," Genina pacified them. "He is only in a bad mood."

"He's unpleasant," Loso whispered.

"Oh, no, Loso. When we meet him again–"

"When will that be?" asked Mena quickly.

"I don't know. Come, children." Genina tore a few young shoots from the bushes. "Eat this, it's wonderfully fresh. And good for you."

They moved forward slowly, enjoying whatever offered itself by the way.

"Mmm!" Mena smacked her lips.

"We should always have things as good as this," was Loso's opinion.

Genina kept still. She was thinking of Rombo.

In front of them the bushes thinned out. The open space of a meadow spread wide before them. Genina slowed her pace, scenting the air carefully.

Above her on a long branch of a tree Perri shrilled, "Here they are!"

Hardly had they stepped out of the brush than they were surrounded by a whole herd of roes.

"Genina! How nice you're alive!... How good to see you again!... I'm glad, Genina!... And *the* beautiful children!... Why, you already have your red summer coats.... Things seem to have gone pretty well with you.... Where have you all been?"

Cheered by the friendly reception, Genina told them, "With Him!"

Full of sudden reserve, they all backed away. One mother roe nudged her kid and both galloped off, frightened.

"Why this fear?" Genina called after them. "You have no reason to be afraid."

An old roe explained gravely: "It's dislike."

"There's no reason for that either."

"It's in our blood," the old roe insisted, "and so it must be right."

"But you don't know Him. You don't know anything about Him. First you must learn to know Him—as we do."

A few pushed closer curiously; the others, gathering courage, pushed no less eagerly after them.

"Tell us about it, Genina. . . . Tell us everything. . . . What a strange adventure you must have had! . . . Did nothing bad happen to you? . . . Or to the young ones?"

Genina told how they had gone down to the Lodge and lived in the stable. None of the roes could grasp what a stable was.

Then Genina remembered a hunting hut that stood in the forest. "You know the hide-out that He built here?"

"You mean that funny thing that never grows? That thing He runs into so as not to be seen?"

"Yes. Well, it's like that but many times bigger. And there are horses inside."

"Horses! How many?"

"Two giant ones, one of them very wild."

"Weren't you or the youngsters ever afraid?"

"Oh, we were frightened often enough," Genina admitted, "for the fiery horse always fought with the cow and the donkey. At least, argued with them."

"What! A cow there too?"

"A donkey too? And who else?"

"No one else. Only the young ones and I. It was wonderfully warm. Outside there was frost and snow, but inside we were cozy."

"Then that's why you already have your summer coats, isn't it?"

"What? Why—probably," Genina said with surprise as though she hadn't thought of it before. "We could go out in the open as often as we felt like it. But the children—" She caught herself up, ashamed. She lifted her head. "Of course we went outdoors all the time. The board that closed the stable moved. All we had to do was lean our foreheads against it–and it turned."

Perri, crouching on the lowest branch, was listening. She whistled. "What a lot of miracles! You need courage for a life like that–full of surprises! You must have been happy too–eh?"

Genina raised her head higher. "Happy–no, I wasn't. I'm happy now. I felt safe, it's true. I knew I wouldn't lose the children to the torture death. But no, it wasn't easy to live that way. Big as it was, that space made me feel–like a prisoner. And then I–I grew afraid the children would lose their love of freedom–"

"What about the others with you there? Aren't they free?"

"No, not at all. They don't even know what freedom is. They *belong* to Him. Even the tomcat, who thinks he's free. They must all obey and serve their master."

"Obey? . . . Serve? . . . Master? . . ." Heads lifted questionably.

Genina shook her ears helplessly. "I don't know how to explain. It's–it's something strange and–terrible. They have no wills of their own."

"What about Him?" demanded the oldest roe. "Is He dreadful?"

"No—and yes," Genina said reflectively. "We shuddered when He came close to us and *touched* us."

"With the thunder-stick?"

"No! He had no thunder-stick. He touched us very gently. With His hands."

"How horrible!"

"Yes, it was horrible. But He didn't harm us. On the contrary, He was very good to us. The most terrible thing is His smell. It drives sorrow and fear into your heart. Flight is your only feeling then."

"But still you *didn't* flee," the oldest roe pointed out.

"We often wanted to. At least—*I* did—" Genina grew confused again. She hurried on. "But in the middle of winter we couldn't. We feared the choking danger in the forest."

"You poor things!"

"Yes, we had to control ourselves. It took a long time until we could even halfway endure that gruesome scent."

"Tell us more!" urged some of the younger roes.

"Later, perhaps. Now we must go on alone." Genina made a lithe leap and called, "Children!"

Mena and Loso, who had been listening demurely, jumped to their mother's side. She ordered, "Forward!"

Swiftly she galloped around the clearing, circling back to their starting place. Breathlessly the twins followed her.

"Ah! That was magnificent, wasn't it? I haven't done that for a long time. *You* never did. Shall we do it again?"

"Yes! Yes!" cried the youngsters.

Again they galloped across the clearing, crisscross, back and forth. Loso and Mena enjoyed the running. They breathed lightly and rejoiced in the young strength of their nimble limbs. They were so caught up by the momentum of their running that they had to spread their forelegs to stop when Genina came to a sudden halt.

From out of the wilted grass the leek pointed its new green leaves. Mena and Loso wanted to get at it; the strong smell tempted them.

"Don't eat any of it," their mother ordered; "it'll make you sick. We'll nibble the fresh shoots at the edge of the thicket instead."

The twins abandoned the leek to stalk slowly behind their mother along the edge of the forest, picking at hazel and elderbushes. They were hungry.

The return of the mother and her offspring was the big event of the forest. Roes joined them one after the other, wanting to hear the tale.

"No more today!" answered Genina again and again. "We're tired. Perhaps tomorrow."

Suddenly two hares sat before them. Their ears high, they begged, "Genina, tell us how it was."

The roe sniffed at them. "And who may you be?"

The hares' ears fell back. "You don't know us?"

"I haven't the slightest idea who you are."

"We were your good friends!" One of them sat up straighter, his mustache hairs almost touching Genina's nostril. "We were *good* friends."

"Anybody can say that," Genina murmured.

Loso and Mena stared at the hares, amazed, for they

could not remember ever having seen them before.

"Have you become proud—snobbish?" the hares demanded.

"No, I'm not proud. I'm just tired," Genina said. "The children and I must eat our fill. Sorry. Please leave us to ourselves."

Timidly the hares made a few long leaps, crouched again and looked back. Their ears played excitedly. They could not understand their dismissal.

"It's just too much," Genina muttered loud enough for them to hear, "to have to answer *every* question."

Tambo stepped out into the clearing. He was some little distance from the roes. They had not yet noticed him and he hesitated to approach them. He still had his yellow-brown winter coat, and his crown, which promised to become mighty, protruded only half-grown. A little behind him was Debina, not daring to come forward.

Perri had told Tambo the amazing tale of Genina and her children. And now he had decided to talk with her himself.

But somehow he felt shy about it. He told himself

how improper it would be to address a stranger. The next moment he took heart and said to himself, "But none of us are strangers to one another." He came up softly and carefully.

When Genina did catch sight of him, she gave a cry of fright and sprang blindly into the bushes. "*Ba-uh!* Quick, children, run away! *Ba-uh! Ba-uh! Ba-uh!*"

In their high little voices Loso and Mena screeched, "*Ba-uh! Ba-uh!*"

Three in a row they plunged through the thicket, driven by blind terror.

"*Ba-uh!*" cried Genina. "*Ba-uh!* Did you see him? *Ba-uh!* One of our big cousins! *Ba-uh!* They're dangerous. *Ba-uh!*"

She could not calm herself. For a long time Tambo could hear her cries of fright. He stood embarrassed and ashamed.

"I'm a fool," he thought. "It was my own fault. I should never have surprised them. I should have known it's impossible for one of our kind to talk with the little relatives. They always dash away in fear. Too bad. We certainly don't want to harm them. They're so nice."

He moved into the forest depths where the bushes grew thickest. Now he was not aware of his imposing appearance, nor of Debina who adored him. He had only the humiliation of feeling shunned. Every far-off cry of Genina's increased his depression. When finally she fell silent, he was relieved.

Genina herself was soon to taste the feeling of being rejected.

Rombo appeared suddenly before her, and as suddenly ran away. The louder she called after him, the faster he went. Resentment flashed through her.

"Stupid buck!" she muttered. "Run, for all I care. Some day you'll want to talk to me again and then *I* won't be in the mood!"

Gently the morning dawned. Through the grill of treetops the sky shimmered a light gray.

"I'm tired," Mena complained.

"How about you?" the mother asked Loso.

"I'm sleepy too," he admitted.

"We'll go home, then, to our own place," Genina decided.

On their way they met many other roes and exchanged brief greetings with them. But nobody stopped, for all were bound for their resting places.

Clapping their wings, awakened pheasants swung from their sleeping-trees to the ground. Their loud *gocking* sounded as if they were trying to crow like roosters, and as if their throats would burst with the effort.

Mena and Loso heard these sounds with surprise. They marveled at the pheasants' magnificence of color, which they had never seen before.

Just before they reached their bed they saw something so disturbing that all sleepiness abruptly left them.

A large pheasant cock was ambling leisurely among the bushes. Suddenly a red hunter sprang on his back, pressing him to the ground. The dying bird lay twitching with powerless wings outspread.

Quaking, the roes slipped by, taking care not to look as the wild one feasted. They hoped he wouldn't notice them.

"Mother, who is that enemy?" Loso asked when they were safe, his voice quivering.

"Is that the fox?" Mena wanted to know. She too still trembled with excitement.

"Yes, children. That's the fox."

"He's horrible!" Mena choked.

"He's powerful—probably the most powerful of the small enemies in the forest."

"And he's beautiful too—" Loso shuddered. "I can't help thinking that."

"Remember what he looks like, children," warned Genina. "Pointed head, sly cruel eyes, bushy tail. Did you breathe his heavy scent? Yes, remember his scent too. Never forget it! And never try to cross his merciless path."

It was broad daylight when the three roes reached the hollow where the twins were born. The magpies chattered, the titmice whispered, the woodpecker hammered, as mother and young ones bedded themselves down.

For a long time they discussed the horrible scene they had witnessed.

Then sleep enveloped them.

Chapter 16

IT WAS TOWARD MORNING WHEN pungent smoke wakened the animals in the stable. Manni sniffed deliberately while Devil and Witch stamped anxiously.

"What's this?" gasped Devil.

"Fire!" said Manni, trying to control his excitement. "In the hayloft over us!"

Panic seized Lisa. She swayed back and forth in her stall, bellowing and pushing the calf from one corner to the other.

"All of you get out in the open!" ordered Manni.
"Let's fetch the two-legged ones!"

He pressed through the swinging doors, the horses
behind him. Even Lisa obeyed him, calling her calf. Outside, pale dawn announced the approaching day. From
the stable eaves little blue and yellow flames licked out.
At the sight Lisa lost her head completely and made an
about-face to run back inside.

Manni blocked her way. "Are you crazy?"

The cow threatened him with lowered horns.

"No farther!" shouted Manni. "Not a step! Go ahead
and gore me, for all I care. But you're not going back
into that fire!"

The stallion stepped between to stop the calf who
had become even more panicky than the mother and
was trying to reach the stable door. Devil snorted at
them both, "Be stupid whenever you want. But not
now—understand? Forward—with us!"

He pushed his forehead into Lisa's flank. She
trembled, seeming to change her mind and have no will
of her own.

"Quick—quick!" the donkey commanded.

Shepherding the cow and calf between them, they galloped to the Lodge.

"The two-legged ones are still asleep," said Manni. "We must wake them up!"

Then the cow and calf bellowed, the horses neighed and the donkey brayed.

Up in their rooms Martin, Peter and Babette leaped out of their beds in alarm.

"What's up?" Martin called to Peter, who was looking out the window while pulling on his clothes.

"The stable's on fire!" Peter shouted back.

"Fire?" Martin cried. "How? What caused—"

"Never mind that now, sir," said Peter. "Let's hurry."

Hastily Martin slipped into his trousers and shirt.

Poor Babette suddenly began to act like Lisa the cow, screaming in terror.

Peter shouted at her. "Quiet! Quiet! Control yourself!"

He and Martin were already among the animals and on their way to the barn.

While the stable creatures had been sounding the alarm at the Lodge, the owl had returned from her nightly hunt to seek her accustomed nesting place in the barn. The flames and the sharp biting smoke frightened her badly. Over the gusts of smoke she floated in soundless flight and disappeared toward the forest hill.

Martin and Peter ran to the barn. Behind them came the horses followed by Lisa and the calf, who were chased in turn by the donkey.

Hastily Peter fetched the hose from the shed, unrolled it and screwed it into the hydrant. Martin turned the water on. A thick stream of water shot up to the roof.

The flames flared up as if to resist, yet presently collapsed and died out. Finally only a few wisps of smoke were spiraling skyward. Then Peter dragged the hose into the barn and drenched the rafters and walls until they dripped.

The hiss of the water shooting from the hose made the horses afraid at first. They reared, then moved a little way off. Excited and nervous, they watched what was going on.

Lisa had fled into the garden with her calf. She could not be seen and only her occasional short groans could be heard. Babette went to calm her. After a while there was silence.

"The fire's under control now," Peter said finally.

Martin said, "Let's wait another hour or so anyway—just to be sure."

"I'd better take a look at the hayloft," Peter decided. He climbed the ladder, and soon he was throwing down bundles of hay, some badly charred, others thoroughly water-soaked.

"Only small damage," Peter called. "The roof has hardly been singed."

As he came down the ladder he said, "Spontaneous combustion. That hay was bone-dry. And the sun beating on the roof all day set it afire. Anyway, we got here in time. When the water dries up, things will be all right again."

"Our good friends here," Martin said, "rescued themselves and saved the stable."

He went to the horses, caressed their throats and heads and talked tenderly.

Peter joined them, and lovingly patted Manni's back. "He was the leader, I'm sure."

He turned to see the stable door standing wide open. "So, friends," he called to the horses and the donkey, "you can move back into your palace again. And here, Lisa—you too, and your calf. Well, Babette," he smiled at his wife who walked behind the cow, "all's well again, you see."

Babette smiled sheepishly and slapped the cow on the flank. "She was even more scared than I was!"

The three trudged back to the house. Glowing a wonderful red, the sun rose into the heavens.

The animals re-entered the stable.

"What a mess!" exclaimed the stallion.

"It certainly isn't very pretty," the mare agreed.

"Everything's wet," Lisa grumbled.

Manni quieted her. "It'll soon dry."

"Soon dry!" Devil mocked him. "What's the good of all this water?"

"To put out the fire," Manni patiently explained.

"The fire! That wasn't bad," the stallion snorted.

"And how it smells here!" the mare complained, her nostrils wrinkling.

"Disgusting!" Devil was indignant.

"The smell will disappear," Manni said earnestly to soothe them.

"Disappear!" raged the stallion. "*You* ought to disappear, you know-it-all!"

"What did the Hes do here, after all?" Witch inquired.

Manni said, "They saved us and the barn."

"What do you mean—'us'?" snorted Devil. "We weren't in any danger. Not for a second!"

"Then why did we go for them?" the donkey demanded. "Why did we call in front of the house until they woke up and came to our aid?" He looked at the cow. "Why was the mother here in such a panic? Why is she now so sure of herself again? Why are you just as calm? Because we still have our living place even though it is a little wet. Because we owe great thanks to our two-legged friends for their quick help. Why don't you admit it?"

The stallion flamed furiously, "Must you *always* be

right?" Frothing, he kicked out blindly and hit the donkey on the throat close to his head.

Manni collapsed to the floor. Blood gushed from his nose and mouth.

Terrified, the mare neighed.

Lisa lowered her horns threateningly at Devil. "You cruel fool! I'd like to gore you!"

The calf begged, "Don't, mother, don't!"

Manni was whispering faintly in a choking voice, "Forgive me, I don't always have to be right. Forgive me…"

But Devil stood stony, desperate, lost. Then he timidly bent over Manni, who was breathing heavily. "*You* forgive *me*. Friend! Good, gentle friend! I didn't want to hurt you. You know how idiotic I am when I get in a rage. But I'm not really bad. Never! Does it hurt much?"

"No," the donkey said in a weak voice, "only at first…." Blood still ran from his neck.

"Can't you stand up?" Devil asked worriedly.

"I'll try, if you wish." Manni could only whisper. He threshed his legs and had to lie on his side. Then he lost consciousness.

"He's asleep," said the stallion, slightly relieved.

But Lisa declared, "He's more than asleep. It's almost like death."

Devil did not dare utter another word; his ears lay flat and dejected.

"This comes from your always getting excited." Witch began to reproach him. She spared him not at all, listing all his outbursts of proud and stupid fury. Lisa chimed in feelingly.

The stallion kept silent, filled with a sense of guilt.

Finally Witch said, "And what if you've killed him? Suppose he dies now?"

"Then—then—I don't want to live either," stammered Devil.

But after an anxious hour, Manni breathed more easily. The bleeding had stopped and he awakened. With great effort he got up shakily.

They surrounded him, Devil with them. "Are you well again? Have you any pain? You're not bleeding any more, are you?"

"Get well," the stallion begged him. "Please get well and I'll show you how much I love you."

"We all love you!" the others chorused.

Manni was deeply moved. "This is rich reward for a trifling injury, but I've learned my lesson. In the future I'll be careful. It's dangerous to be too wise. It's even more dangerous to talk wisely before you're asked your opinion."

Chapter 17

THE SUMMER SUN BLAZED FROM
the heavens. So glowing hot were the days
that the air seemed to boil. And the nights
were steaming.

In this orgy of sun the forest creatures enjoyed
increased well-being and a mounting joy in life. From
the very break of day the pheasants clucked, the magpies and jays chattered, the woodpecker hammered
more industriously than ever. The glittering kingfisher
zoomed like a flash through the air. The water wagtails,

with their long narrow bobbing tails, rocked themselves in low flight or else strolled elegantly on the banks of the streams with friendly nods.

High in the blue above the fields where crops were ripening for harvest, the jubilant larks trilled without stopping.

In the forest the cuckoo called out his roguish challenge, luring the female who flittered coyly around him.

The oriole flew from the tree, uttering his short glad song. The finches sang their beautiful poem, punctuated by their mysterious *Psst! Psst!*

The blackbirds hacked and drilled after earthworms, but found none because of the drought. Disappointed, they tried out various new cadences in their morning and evening songs.

The squirrels dashed gaily along the branches, gathering beechnuts and hazelnuts. They gobbled greedily or else added them to their secret reserve supplies, which they later often forgot.

The roebucks began courting the does. Here and there one pursued the doe he was wooing across a meadow and through the thicket. The does fled, sometimes in earnest flight, sometimes coquettishly. Yet here and there one of them sounded her delicate, longing peep because she was lonely and wanted to let her suitor know where she was.

Now the mothers seemed to lose all interest in their children. The abandoned young tripped through bushes and meadow plaintively calling for the once faithful guardians who had so bewilderingly failed in their duty. They had no idea why they were deserted. This was their first bitter experience of life.

Even Arilla, who still mourned her husband—the dangerous murderer with the long daggerlike horns whom Peter had destroyed—even Arilla was courted now by new swains.

"Come with me," one of them offered. "You mustn't be sad."

"Be mine, Arilla," urged another. "I love you."

"Listen to me," begged a third. "I admired you even when your ruffian was alive."

"Don't say such things to me," whispered Arilla.

"Why not?" they demanded. "This widowhood must end. Everyone will laugh at you. You're being silly. Be gay, Arilla! We're just as good as he was. No—we're *better*!"

"You're wrong," Arilla countered softly. "I don't want any of you. No one can replace him."

She had hardly finished saying this when a mighty buck stormed up like a hurricane and took her away before him.

Gone was Arilla's sadness. She thought nothing, resisted no more, felt only happiness that a new master now dominated her. Soon she followed him obediently, away from the others.

With her children, Genina was wandering indifferently along the familiar trails. Yet in her heart there still beat longing for Rombo: the wish that he might again be with her as he had been long ago.

Hah-ah-hahaha-ah! came the melancholy song of the great gray owl. Soundlessly she flew close to the heads of the three roes.

"Greetings. How are you?" asked Genina, glad to be diverted by conversation.

"Oh," answered the owl, "now that I'm away from Him, I have nothing evil to fear."

"Away from Him? But you were so friendly with Him!"

"But *you* left Him too."

"Yes," Genina admitted, "because spring came. Because we longed again for the forest. But we didn't leave for fear of evil!"

"Then you were lucky."

"And what happened to you?"

The owl snapped her beak angrily. "Nothing! I was lucky too, I must say. Lucky and wise. Listen. One morning I was coming home to my quiet little place, and what do I find? Everything full of smoke, smell and fire! No horses, no donkey, no cow, no calf. The entire place empty. It was a trap for me—you see? But they didn't get me. Not me! Oh, He's treacherous and tricky. You can't trust Him."

Genina said with surprise, "Really, I can hardly believe that!"

The owl insisted, still snapping her beak, "You can believe me all right!"

Genina objected: "He was always good and kind to us."

"Yes," the owl continued with sage nods. "He pretended . . . but only to win our confidence. And then—"

"You see, mother," Loso said, "I was right to be afraid."

"And my fear," Mena added, "wasn't so foolish either."

"See what happened," Loso continued triumphantly, "to the good owl."

"Always listen to children," said the owl. "They have a sure instinct. Farewell!" And she flew away.

Genina stared after her, confused and troubled. Then suddenly she saw Rombo approaching, slowly, looking friendly. Love and resentment struggled in Genina's breast.

"Rombo!" she whispered rapturously. "Rombo!"

Loso and Mena stood still, except for their ears which waggled joyfully.

Genina recovered herself. "Don't you pay any

attention to your father," she ordered. "No greeting. And don't move from my side."

Rombo strutted toward her, his legs lifting nobly. "Greetings, Genina!"

She made a sulky face and was silent.

But Loso called out, "Greetings, father!"

"We've been waiting for you so long!" Mena said tenderly.

Genina looked at them in annoyance.

But Rombo was very gentle. "How pretty they are, those two! My compliments, Genina."

She was still silent.

"Why don't you speak to me?" Rombo said softly. "The children are nice to me, but you—"

"You don't deserve friendliness," she retorted. "You faithless—"

"I was not! I was only hurt—"

"You behaved badly, Rombo. Very badly."

"Because you abandoned me, Genina."

"You should have been happy to see me again."

"I was. But I didn't want you to know."

"And now suddenly you do?" Genina was skeptical.

"Yes, Genina. I'm not angry with you anymore. And you must forgive me."

"Must you talk in front of the children?" she asked, already half won over.

"Be off with you—immediately!" he commanded the children. "I want to be alone with your mother." Frightened, Mena and Loso rushed away. "They're almost grown up," he declared. Then he spoke firmly: "Now it's just as it used to be. We're together again. . . ."

Chapter 18

IN THE AUTUMN THE STAGS HAD SHED their crowns. Many a helpless hazel bush, many a young birch and ash had lost their bark under their butting blows. First the naked wood stared out, white-yellow; then it was veined with red, and finally it showed open and discolored wounds. Many a bush and a few trees died slowly from the scars made by the stately stags' antlers.

During the shedding season, Debina had waited at a little distance from Tambo.

Now she admired her chosen one's superb violence and the growing beauty of his new crown. It had fourteen ivory-colored points.

It was the mating season again, and Debina's presence embarrassed Tambo. She still followed him modestly and silently, pacing behind him on his secret winding paths, sleeping nearby when he rested, rising when he rose. She never realized she might be intruding, never thought she might be a burden to him.

Often Tambo intended to ask her to leave him alone, not to follow him anymore. But he could not find the right way to speak to her. Then he had begun to realize that if he drove her away, he would miss her. He saw how used to her he had grown. So he said nothing.

One day when Debina was sleeping soundly, Tambo, who never allowed himself the luxury of deep sleep, heard His steps coming closer and closer.

Martin was out for a walk. He was not seeking Tambo's bed, nor would he have disturbed it. Softly the stag rose and slipped away very quietly, at first moving slowly, then faster and faster. Finally, he shot off like an arrow. Sometimes he paused to listen. He could still hear His steps.

Tambo zigzagged into the distance. Then he heard other movements. Frightened, he threw back his head and scented the breeze. The noise of the other feet was plain.

Peter was following Martin. He caught up with him and their steps sounded together.

Panic overcame Tambo. He ran farther and farther without knowing why. As the wind shifted, he caught the scent of both the two-legged ones. Thoroughly alarmed now, he did not remember their past goodness. He didn't think at all. He rushed blindly to the most distant boundary of the hunting preserve where the cultivated fields began. But so well did he instinctively control himself, that even his mad rush was noiseless. Through the densest thicket his hoofs made no sound. Finally he stopped and listened carefully. Now he heard no steps. He scented the air in all directions. It was clear. Again, as once before, a happy feeling of liberation shot through him. It glowed warmly in him.

Only then did he remember Debina. Had he lost her? Had he escaped her too? Was he rid of her? His first thought was that he was glad. His burden was gone.

But he became sad again at once. Why, he could not do without her!

Debina awoke with a feeling that something must have gone wrong with Tambo. His bed was empty. The trail he had left was barely visible. The scent which might have guided her to him was blown away by the wind.

She set out in sad confusion to look for him. Lacking courage to run, she went step by step, stopped, stood without moving, inhaled the air questioningly. Nothing.

She started blaming herself, longing and worrying. How could she have slept? It was frivolous to sleep and wake too late. What had happened to her friend and master? No one would dare attack him. The thunderstick had not thundered, and so–

Yet He had soundless weapons too, Debina knew–a mysterious power strong enough to murder even the mighty Tambo. Debina did not give a thought to His goodness. All her confidence disappeared. She grew desperate.

A sharp, unpleasant scent caught her attention. The fox! He slunk by quite close to her, and she forced herself to call to him.

"Greetings."

Surprised, the fox stopped. "Were you speaking to me?"

"Yes, Red Robber!"

The fox crooked a foreleg breast high. A sarcastic smile twisted his wily face. "Aren't you afraid of me?"

"When I was small and weak, I was," Debina said. "But I've not been for a long time now."

"Proud one!" grinned the fox. "You had a royal protector until—" he hesitated, slyly.

"Until—? Well, speak up!" Debina pressed him.

"Until he deserted you."

She was speechless. It had not occurred to her that Tambo had gone just to get rid of her. Now she believed it at once. Ashamed, helpless, filled with mourning, she dropped her head.

The fox was sorry for her. "Don't take it so hard! I said that only as a joke because you hurt me."

Debina looked up quickly. "How?"

"You called me 'robber.'"

"Aren't you proud of being a robber?"

"I don't know. Have you any idea, you happy grass-eater, what a life I lead? How much hunger I suffer? What dangers threaten me? How I risk my neck again and again? How much presence of mind it takes to save myself? And how wearying it is? If I could satisfy my appetite as easily as you and your kind, I wouldn't have to slip around stealthily, or be ready to flee at every moment. My flight would be as free and open as Tambo's."

"Do you know anything about Tambo?"

"Indeed I do," said the fox. "I know everything."

"Tell me!" urged Debina.

"He fled for no reason, like a coward." And the fox recounted the story of Tambo's fear and flight. "By the way, aren't you going the wrong way?" And he directed her in the course Tambo had taken.

Debina started off immediately. But the fox blocked her way. She almost stepped on him. She was annoyed. "What does this mean? Don't delay me."

Politely he retorted, "That's exactly my intention."

Debina stamped with her strong forelegs. "Go away!"

The fox smiled, still more suavely polite. "You'll have to learn patience."

"*Have* to!" she burst out. "You're impudent! If you think you can order me—"

"Now just look." His politeness remained smooth, but was mixed with irony. "How bossy you are! Yes, yes—only a moment ago you listened to my confession with sympathy. I'd have thought we were friends."

"There can be no friendship between us! You know that."

"I know that," he repeated lightly. "Still, I told you about Tambo, and showed you how to find him."

Debina nodded.

"And now," continued the fox, "you leave me without thanks, without a parting word. Your behavior isn't nice at all—not at all."

Embarrassed, Debina asked, "My thanks mean something to you?"

The fox's tail drooped. "In all the forest I have no friends," he said. "Not a single one. All are my enemies and I'm the enemy of all. Sometimes I hate this . . ."

"Only you yourself are to blame," Debina admonished him. Against her will, the red robber at her feet fascinated her.

"Your greeting," the fox admitted, "touched my poor lonely heart and made me weak. Now you can measure how great value your thanks would have for me . . ."

"Then–then I thank you. And farewell!"

"Very nice," the fox murmured. "No friendship. But even bare friendliness feels good."

"Now let me go," Debina demanded, impatient again. "You've delayed me too long already."

"I'm not delaying you, Debina. I'm helping you," the fox replied. "Take my advice. I mean it well. Don't run, don't hurry. Stroll slowly, calmly. Then you won't frighten Tambo when he sees you. Farewell!"

In a flash the fox vanished. Only his evil scent

stayed for a while in Debina's nostrils. For a second she stood still, then started off as the fox had directed her, step by step on Tambo's trail, never attempting a cross-cut. From time to time she paused to listen.

She was subdued. She wanted only to think of Tambo. His kingly dignity did not suffer in her eyes even when she remembered that he had fled "like a coward."

"What was degrading about that?" she asked herself. "Nothing at all!" When He came into the forest—He whom none could resist, whose power was without limit, whose intentions could not be guessed—then, yes, then even Tambo might flee.

She saw nothing and caught no scent. She began to suspect that the fox had deceived her. This made her doubly helpless. Swiftly she turned and sprang in the opposite direction. But only for a little way. Almost at once she stopped and told herself, "No, the fox didn't fool me. Impossible! What he said rang true."

Believing it now firmly, she turned around again and proceeded slowly, sometimes with the wind, then against it, as it shifted from time to time. Suddenly a faint breath of Tambo wafted into her nostrils. It was only for a second, yet Debina gained new life from it.

Now she knew! "Tambo is near! Tambo is coming!"

She pressed on through a birch grove that was bare of underbrush and very light.

On the far side of this grove appeared a figure. Tambo! He lifted his head and saw her. She stood still, caught again by the majesty of his crown, the richness of his mane, the beauty of his body.

Tambo began a gallop toward her. His bearing spoke his joy.

Happily Debina galloped toward him. Then, at her old accustomed distance, she stopped, humbly still.

At once Tambo slowed to a walk and paced by her.

Devotedly she turned to follow him, and with that he seemed content.

Now he sought a new bed. At length, in the densest part of the thicket, he found a suitable camping place. Very tired, he let himself down full length.

Some distance away Debina found another bed.

The two of them had not spoken a syllable, nor exchanged greetings. Yet both derived a tender and pleasant peace from each other's presence.

Tambo fell asleep immediately.

But Debina stayed awake, watching him. She was thinking with sympathy of the fox.

Chapter 19

IN THE STABLE THINGS HAD CHANGED.

Manni the donkey was still weak and they all worried over him. But if they asked, "How goes it with you?" he always answered, "Very well, thank you."

Yet in truth it did not go well with him at all.

Timid and ashamed, Devil was the one most anxious about him. Devil too had changed. He was more gentle and patient, and no longer had fits of anger. He made every effort to get Manni to talk, always seeking his opinion. Yet on every topic Manni kept silent or said only, "I don't know," or, "That's beyond me."

Lisa was nicest of all. "Drink some of my milk, Gray," she suggested. "It will do you good."

"Thank you, mother," Manni answered, "but I'm not thirsty."

"Drink without thirst then," Lisa urged, "for your health's sake."

"But I don't like milk," Manni protested.

"Try it," whispered the stallion.

Without answering, Manni, his gait uncertain, walked through the swinging doors into the garden.

"He hasn't forgiven me yet," whinnied Devil.

"Oh yes, he has! He forgave you right after you kicked him," Witch consoled him. "But leave him alone. Don't ask him so many questions. Don't give him so much advice. Peace is all he wants."

"Maybe you're right," the stallion admitted readily. These days he agreed with everyone.

The donkey, tired and sick, stood outside in the sun. It was hard for him to breathe. His throat and head hurt badly.

Witch and Devil came out to join him.

"It's nice here," Devil remarked, to start conversation.

Manni nodded silently.

"Do you remember the roes we had here?"

Again a silent nod.

"You never really told us about your adventures in the forest," the stallion said gently.

"Oh, yes, I did," said Manni.

"Not enough," the stallion urged.

Manni kept silent.

"You promised us more later," Witch whispered, forgetting the advice she had given Devil.

"Did I? I don't remember."

The mare adopted a new tone. "Listen, Gray, this fellow here"—she indicated Devil with her head—"thinks you haven't forgiven him yet."

"Nonsense!"

"Please tell him that you forgive—"

"No!"

"Then he's right?"

"No!"

"But if you did forgive him, couldn't you say it again?"

"No!" The donkey's stubbornness broke out. He turned away and swayed back into the barn. The horses followed him sadly.

"What's the matter?" Lisa wanted to know.

She received no answer from Manni, but Witch in whispers described the scene and the stallion's sorrow.

"That's just Gray's way," the cow observed. "He said once that he forgave Devil. Now he acts as if he hadn't. Don't worry about it, fiery one." She still called Devil that though now he was anything but fiery. "And anyway, look at Gray. He really feels badly."

The donkey was leaning against the wall and groaning.

The horses hurried over to him. "How do you feel?"

Manni answered softly, "Very well, thank you."

"Aren't you feeling bad?"

"No."

"Do you have pain?"

"No."

Peter entered the stable with the veterinarian. He

was explaining. "Two weeks ago he was in sound health. But now see there, Doctor."

"Why, he's wasting away!" the veterinarian exclaimed.

"Exactly!" Peter nodded.

The veterinarian went toward Manni, who backed away stubbornly.

"What's the matter with you, Manni?" In his gentle way Peter caressed the donkey's neck, but accidentally on the sore spot.

Manni's teeth snapped, and Peter might have been bitten had he not quickly pulled back his hand.

He was startled. "Poor fellow! He must be very ill. I've never seen him so angry."

Remorsefully Manni laid his head against Peter's breast. Touched, the old man murmured, "Yes, boy, yes. Now we're friends again, aren't we?" To the veterinarian he whispered: "Now, Doctor, quickly and thoroughly!" He caressed Manni's forehead and cheeks, while he covered the donkey's eyes with his hands.

The doctor tapped Manni's lungs, flanks and kidney region. Manni bore it stolidly.

"Now," said the veterinarian, "I'd like to look into his mouth. Will he stand for it?"

"If I open his mouth, certainly." Peter took hold of the silky soft jowls. "Now, Manni, now. It'll be all over in just a moment."

Good-naturedly Manni opened his jaws. The doctor glanced in quickly. "Nothing, not a trace of illness" was his judgment. "As far as I can see, there is not a thing the matter with him."

"But his condition is pitiful," Peter complained. "It's strange—and puzzling."

The veterinarian shrugged helplessly. Both men departed.

"They are stupid," Lisa muttered.

The stallion neighed softly, "They have the best intentions."

"What good is that?" grumbled Lisa. "What good is that if one's as stupid as straw?"

The mare was more hopeful. "Now that the Hes have touched him, perhaps it'll go better with Gray."

Devil agreed. "We don't understand what they do. But they can do so much."

"They can't do anything, the dumb things." Lisa was stubborn. "All our misfortune comes from their not understanding us and our not understanding them."

The stallion agreed with her then. "Yes, giver of milk, that's true. We can only half understand, half guess what they mean."

"Half?" The cow shook her broad head. "That would be a lot. All we can do is guess a tiny bit, no more. And what do they understand about us? Almost nothing."

"Oh, you're unfair," Devil objected. "They probably understand more than you think. They're very good to us, after all."

"They guess a lot of things, too," the cow put in, "but it amounts to very little in the end. And *ours* are exceptions. All the others treat our kind brutally. Cruelly! Outrageously!"

The stallion begged, "Don't say that!"

"And don't exaggerate so," the mare added.

"I'm not exaggerating," the cow argued. "What I say is true, and only a small part of the truth."

"If you're right," the stallion replied, "how very lucky we are!"

"Yes, as long as everything runs smoothly." The cow's tail whipped her flanks. "But look at Gray and see if you still think we're lucky."

"It's my fault," sighed the stallion, "all my own fault."

"Yes, it's your fault," repeated the cow. "But now if we could talk with Him—discuss things with Him just as we talk among ourselves—"

"Hopeless," whispered Witch.

"—then maybe," Lisa completed her thought, "Gray could be saved."

Manni was standing with trembling knees, holding groans back by sheer force of will.

"How do you feel, friend?" the stallion inquired for the thousandth time.

"Thank you, quite well," Manni answered in a barely audible voice.

Chapter 20

FTER THE EXCITEMENT OF THE
mating season had subsided, Rombo
became himself again. Though he still
was fond of Genina, he began more and
more to wander around alone, to graze alone, and to
rest alone.

Nor did Genina feel so dependent on his presence
as she had a few weeks before. She, too, was satisfied to
be by herself.

Accidentally she met Arilla one day.

Still dazed and dreamy, Arilla recounted how her new mate had driven her brutally away from him.

"Do you like such brutality?" Genina asked in wonder.

"*Like?* What a weak expression, Genina!"

"I don't understand."

"But, Genina, the second was the same kind of ruffian buck as my unforgettable one! Now do you understand?"

"No."

With some impatience, Arilla said, "I thought my first could never be replaced. But the second completely replaced him."

"Was he just as good to you?"

"Nonsense!" Arilla preened herself. "Any of them can be good to you. That's nothing!"

"Then what else gives you pleasure, Arilla?"

"To have a master. You see, Genina, I want to be dominated—tyrannized over. Then *I* can be devoted. And I'm delighted when my mate puts up with my devotion reluctantly. Or even if he spurns me."

Genina was amazed.

"Understand, Genina, they're just pretending. Really they want loving attention. They expect it. I don't say they long for it. But I love this pretended indifference."

Genina came to a decision. "Arilla, I don't think we can be friends. We're very badly suited to each other. I'll never understand you, nor you me. Farewell." She turned away and went off.

Arilla was baffled. "Silly thing," she said finally to herself. "She has no idea of love—not a glimmer. In all the forest, I'm the only one who knows what love is!"

Now again Genina remembered her children; she had sought them out two or three times of late. To her surprise, Mena, now a dainty hind, had become a coquette. Loso, a charming little single-horned buck, flirted amusingly, clumsily, with does much older than he.

The delight of this new freedom had been revealed to them both. They no longer waited for Genina to come to them, as they had once upon a time. They no longer needed her motherly leadership. Now they

understood that they were grown up and took a ridiculous pride in the fact.

Genina was halted by a cry. "Mother—greetings!" It
was Mena. Surprised and delighted, she looked at her
daughter. "Greetings, Mena!" Here was no longer a fawn
but a young doe. "How beautiful you are, Mena. How
wonderfully beautiful!"

The young deer glowed with naïve pride. "You really
think so, mother?"

"Yes, and it makes me happy to tell you so, my dear."

Mena laughed, moving her ears. She came closer to
her mother, lightly touched her flank with her muzzle
and whispered, "Oh, not a few have told me that since
you've been gone."

Genina was frightened. "You haven't accepted any
of your suitors?"

Mena leaped mockingly away, came back and
laughed. "You'd like to know, wouldn't you?"

"Don't joke," Genina insisted seriously. "Answer me!"

Mena too became serious then. "No, I haven't."

Genina nodded, satisfied.

"Is there anything else you want to know, mother?"

"Where can I find your brother?"

"That's too much for me!" Mena laughed. "I've been wandering alone for days now."

"Loso doesn't protect you?"

Mena was amused. "I don't need Loso to look after me. I protect myself."

"You don't know where he is now?"

"I haven't the faintest idea."

"Come. We'll look for him together."

They walked along, chatting occasionally or moving in silence, feeling closer to each other than ever before.

Over them floated the great owl. "If I'm not mistaken, you lived with Him."

"Yes," Genina said. "Now I'm looking for my son."

"You haven't far to look," chattered the owl. "Where the three ash trees stand in that tiny clearing. He's there now. Oh, he behaves very well and wisely. You'll hardly recognize him, he's grown so much in the last few weeks. In fact, he's almost better looking than your daughter."

Genina was grateful. She wanted to run to the clearing. But the owl went on, "Really, one ought to be amazed at how quickly youngsters grow up. But every year it's the same. I've seen it so often I'm not surprised anymore."

Genina waited politely, though impatiently, for the wise bird to take her leave. "Well, don't let me delay you," she murmured, and sailed away.

"Let's hurry," Genina exclaimed. But Mena was already leaping ahead of her.

Presently they slowed their pace and stepped delicately, as if in stately dance, into the glade.

Loso looked up, motionless. Then: "Mother," he called very softly.

As softly Genina whispered, "My child."

"You're almost a stranger to me, mother."

"Come to me, Loso. We'll soon know each other again."

"As we did before?" said Loso a little sadly. "No, never again."

Mena threw in snippily, "Is your sister a stranger to you too?"

"Well, Mena"–Loso took on a very superior air–"to tell the truth, you bore me."

Genina asked sorrowfully, "Don't you love each other anymore?"

"I still have a certain liking for you and Mena," Loso said.

"Well, I have very little for you, Loso," Mena retorted, tossing her head. "As for mother, of course I love her, but–she's *funny!*"

Genina's heart beat thickly in her throat. "Am I? To you too, Loso?"

Loso looked away before he said, "Nothing is quainter than a mother who acts as if she were still necessary."

"You don't need me at all?"

"No!" said Loso brusquely.

"Need you?" answered Mena. "No, we don't *need* you. But it makes me happy to go around with you."

"And you, Loso, does it make you happy too?"

"I'd like it very much, mother–now and then."

"Well, my children–" Genina controlled her feelings– "you *have* changed."

"Why did you leave us alone?" Mena asked.

"Because your father–"

"Never mind"–Loso interrupted her–"probably we'd have left you sooner or later anyway. After all, we're grown up."

"But, children, you–"

"Don't call us *children*! We aren't children anymore!" Mena snapped.

"So?" Genina's head lifted high. "Then what shall you call me? Can you ever give me another name? Can I ever stop being your mother? And for me–for me– even if you were ever so old, ever so grown up–for me you'll always be children. My children!"

There was a long pause. Then Mena caressed Genina's throat with her muzzle. Softly, Loso pressed his tiny horns into his mother's flank.

Chapter 21

THE AUTUMN RAIN FELL STEADILY
with a rustling sound. The singing of the
birds ceased. Gusty wind howled through
the treetops and tossed the bushes so that
their leaves dropped soggily to the ground.

When the rain stopped, and the wind was still, the
leaves dried and falling made a soft whisper throughout the forest.

Then came a night when light frost settled over the
hills and glades. But as the sun rose, the shimmering

white disappeared again. Yet the air remained cool. The sun appeared later and later each morning, no longer radiating summer warmth.

But the stags grew livelier. From here and there came their deep groaning bellows. The first one to sound the call of the season was Tambo. His mighty voice roared like thunder.

"Here, to me!" he ordered Debina.

But she had already come close to him. "I am yours," she whispered, "yours forever."

"Yes!" He spoke masterfully, as if in anger.

Modestly his faithful little follower accepted his rule—modestly and happily. "I thank you, Tambo! I love you!"

"Others will belong to me too," Tambo warned her. "You will have to be patient."

"As you command, my lord," she murmured humbly.

"Don't call me yours!" he grumbled. "You are mine. But I am not yours."

"I know," Debina whispered. "Forgive me."

His heavily maned neck stretched out so that his crown of fourteen points lay flat against his back. He bellowed resoundingly. His breath, a gray-white cloud of vapor, floated over his head.

Other does had gathered close by. A few waited in the thicket for Tambo to fetch them. Roughly, quickly, he herded them all together, ten in all, some very young ones among them.

"I will not need to guard you, Debina," he whispered to her. "You are faithful!"

Debina was silent. When she saw no other so noble, could she be anything but faithful?

"But *these*," Tambo rumbled, ready to fight, "—a gallivanting, faithless crowd. I must watch them and see that they do not leave me for any other."

He could sense the presence of other stags, waiting, watching. He could sense the awareness of the does, and their readiness to be won away.

His battle-cry resounded louder and more threatening, more challenging.

Now a young doe tried to slip away into the thicket. Swiftly Tambo caught her and smashed his crown down on her back and flanks. Her legs buckled.

Debina saw a stag come toward Tambo with unwise daring. The newcomer was neither so strong nor so large as Tambo.

Tambo saw him at the same moment, broke off his roaring, and was upon his foe like a storm. Too late the smaller stag turned to flee. With a mighty impact Tambo ran him down. The poor fellow rolled over like a rabbit, his shoulder torn and bloody. Swiftly he picked himself up and limped away.

But during Tambo's momentary absence desertions from his following had already taken place. Three had tried to slip away. Tambo hunted out the three and chased them back into his group. He roared dangerously, with new anger, sending one battle challenge after another into the air. But this time no interloper accepted his challenge.

Admiring, yet painfully perturbed, Debina watched her hero. It was not jealousy that tortured her. She did not misunderstand him. What he did, she felt, he had to do. It just had to be. Not for a moment did she think of rebelling against it. Yet it seemed silly to her that

Tambo should be acting as if his life were at stake. That the kingly Tambo, who had such great dignity, should now behave without any dignity at all—this seemed stranger and stranger to her.

Those coquettish females who had no genuine feeling for him—were they worth guarding so jealously? Worth fetching back when they tried to run off? Worth dominating in so lordly yet so foolish a manner? Were they worth all that?

From time to time sounded the bellowing and roaring of the five or six other Kings who ruled in the forest. Debina wondered if they too behaved in the same senseless way. No doubt, she decided, for Tambo was a King among Kings.

The mating season was at its height for five or six days. Besides the trumpeting of the Kings the forest rang with the high lamentation of the weaker stags who could not find mates.

On the eighth and ninth days Debina felt a piercing sadness, as if she must take leave of something dear which was dissolving before her eyes like a dream. She fought against the feeling with all her inner strength.

Tambo no longer seemed to her a King. He was no longer shining, majestic, proud, but fought-out and tired. Debina reproached herself, but her proud loyalty and intense devotion were gone.

The mating season passed. The does scattered to all directions of the wind. The stags were mute again and the stronger ones slept now, the sleep of the tired warrior.

Tambo too went to seek a bed of rest.

Worried, Debina watched to see if he would recognize her presence as before. She waited for some sign; a look, or even so little as a turn of his crowned head.

Nothing. Dully he passed her as if she were a complete stranger. And she let him pass, neither knowing where he would camp, nor following him.

Very softly she whispered, "Good-by, Tambo."

Then she walked slowly away through the thicket, alone.

Chapter 22

MARTIN WAS CARESSING THE sick donkey and talking to him.

"Manni! My good, fine Manni! Don't do this to me. Get well again, Manni, I beg you!"

Peter and Babette stood by helpless. Martin visited the donkey often and as often imagined he saw signs of improvement. But now, on a rainy cold autumn day, there was no mistaking the truth. Manni could stand erect only by leaning against the wall for support.

He had no stall of his own, for he had never needed one. He had always been undemanding. Often he had slept in the open, or spent the coldest winter nights lying outside the cow's or the horses' stalls. He had never been a burden to anyone, but had always brought them joy. He had guided his stable companions, whose victim he now was, with his ripe wisdom. He had endeared himself to the human beings with his willingness to serve, cheerful if sometimes whimsical and erratic.

Now he could find no place to lie down and be comfortable and he wanted to so very much. He leaned against the wall, his head hanging low.

The hunchback went on talking to him. "Show me your eyes, Manni, your beautiful wise eyes." He lifted the donkey's head gently. "Your eyes are cloudy, my poor friend."

As always Manni laid his chin on Martin's hump and now nuzzled his cheeks with feverish lips. Martin offered him a piece of sugar. "There, there, old chap. There. You always liked that."

Good-manneredly Manni took the tidbit, but let it fall.

"Come, sir," Peter urged.

"Yes, let's go," Babette begged in a whisper. "A sick animal wants only to be left alone."

Once outside the barn Martin broke out, "How could the veterinarian say there's nothing wrong with Manni? The man's an utter ignoramus. Please, Peter, send to the animal hospital. A head doctor must come out. We should have sent for one a long time ago."

Peter excused himself. "We hoped Manni'd get well again, because the veterinarian insisted he was really in good shape." He shook his head. "It's too late now."

The horses, the cow, the calf were disturbed by the strange something that emanated from Manni.

"The two-legged minds have said their farewell to him," mooed Lisa quietly, almost to herself.

"They'll never see Gray alive again," Witch whispered over her stall partition to the cow.

The stallion caught the last words and neighed. "No, Gray, you can't do that to me! No, Gray, you must live! Say you'll live! Don't be so stubborn and silent!"

Manni's head hung even lower, his nose almost touching the barn floor. He said nothing.

Devil raved without restraint. "Don't drive me to distraction, Gray! Have pity on me!"

"You want pity, you murderer?" Lisa burst out. She kept her voice low only with difficulty. "Have pity yourself and grant the dying one a peaceful end."

"*Dying?*" The stallion lost all control. "You miserable milk-giver! I'd like to—" He kicked so that the dividing wall shook.

"Would you, indeed?" roared the cow. "You'd kill me, as you killed him! But I'm not so helpless as poor Gray. Try it and we'll see which of us two—"

"No!" Devil cried shuddering. "No, I won't hurt you! Forgive me. I'll never hurt anyone after this—no one! And Gray—I didn't murder him. I didn't strike him on purpose. Believe me—not on purpose."

"You're so absurd—you and your arrogant idiotic fury." Lisa still assailed him, but was pacified somewhat.

The mare begged, "Don't quarrel now."

"Certainly not," the stallion reassured her. "No quarrels. Right, mother?"

"Right," the cow mooed softly. "But I must be free to speak my opinion."

"Please do." Devil was very meek now.

"I really don't think you meant to kill Gray."

"Thank you, mother. You know I was innocent."

"Oh, no, by no means innocent. You were always in a rage because Gray was smarter than you."

Before anyone else could speak, Manni fell to the floor. Horrified, they all leaped toward him, stood around him.

"Are you feeling bad, Gray?" whimpered the stallion.

To their surprise Manni answered in a clear voice: "Bad? Oh, no! I feel light, wonderfully light . . ."

"Good! Good!" the stallion rejoiced. "That's the beginning, Gray."

"Quiet," the cow warned him. "It's the beginning–of the end!"

Frightened, Devil kept quiet.

Manni's head swept back and forth on the floor. He sighed, "Oh, how beautiful the forest is–how fragrant–"

Understandingly, the mare entered his delirium.

"Whom do you meet in the forest, little Manni?"

"Whom do I not meet? Tambo, you magnificent stag . . . Tambo, I'm not afraid of you. We're friends after all." Manni's voice grew weaker. "Oh, the three nice roes are here again. Welcome—welcome!" Now he was whispering indistinctly. "Don't be afraid—of the Fiery One—he won't hurt you—he is—really—" Then louder again: "Oh, He—"

A shudder ran through Manni's body. He stretched and then lay still.

Chapter 23

SPRING FOUGHT ITS WAY BACK TO the countryside only after long delay and great effort. Chilly weather persisted with its wintry breath. The sky and the earth seemed cut off from each other.

But though gray clouds still masked the sun, the trees began to sprout delicate young leaves. Bitter-cold rain poured down, yet the grass sprouted afresh and the flowers bloomed. Icy winds swept through the forest, but the migrating birds returned joyfully, built their nests and sang as if it were really spring.

The roebucks grew their new horns and would soon be rubbing off their coverings. Their red summer coats, however, were not yet growing properly, so that they went around in off-colored dress from which thick tufts of hair hung loose.

The same thing happened to the coats of the great stags, who looked very shabby. They had lived through the winter in herds, once again experiencing the shame of bald heads. Now their crowns sprouted anew, looking fantastically magnified by the covering.

Tambo's crown rose slowly, but to great height. It was almost ready to give him the delight of rubbing it off.

He too now walked alone. A dark feeling filled him: a vague memory that kept dissolving into nothing, yet tugged at his heart until it hurt. There was something lacking for him. He wondered what it was.

It was loneliness from which he suffered. And he had nothing to confirm his dignity and majesty, his rule over the others. He became irritable, attacked those who crossed his path and was glad the other stags kept away from him. For a while it amused him to frighten roe-bucks and does, to chase and threaten horrified fawns. He became the menace of the forest.

Then, just as quickly, he felt bored, and ashamed of doing such silly things. He resumed the proud gentleness better suited to his nature.

Finally the sunshine and warmth of real spring triumphed. The singing of the birds took on a truer tone. The throbbing of the finches, the rejoicing of the orioles, the calls of the cuckoos, filled the forest with happiness. The squirrels dashed gaily along the branches. The magpies loquaciously chattered all kinds of stories. And the titmice whispered in the bushes.

Gnats danced from early morning till late evening, only to sink down dying at night to make place for new generations. Butterflies, drunk with light, flitted over sunny meadows.

Bumblebees and beetles dashed and whizzed through the air. "Those butterflies," said a fat beetle to his son, "are flowers that have liberated themselves."

"Well, well!" answered the youngster. "Of all things!"

Then a bird snapped up the father in flight. The young-ster simply repeated, "Well, well! Of all things!" He lighted on a leaf and crawled thoughtfully upward to the branch. "I must be careful."

A magpie came to Tambo as the stag was selecting a bedding place. "Are you alone?"

"Yes," Tambo admitted, "I'm all alone."

"That's good," the magpie chattered. "It suits you."

Tambo was silent, for he realized that this solitude suited him in fact very little. He had been used to something different. But he could not remember what and sank to pondering.

"Don't you like to gossip with me?" the magpie asked after a pause.

"No," Tambo retorted brusquely.

"You've become very rude," the magpie remarked and flew away.

Tambo lay down. The early light shimmered and he was sleepy.

Close overhead Perri the squirrel sat on a low shak-ing maple branch. "Greetings, Tambo."

The great stag looked up, "Greetings."

"All alone, Tambo?"

"You can see for yourself."

"Where is—yes, where's Debina?"

Tambo sprang up. *That* was the name he had been seeking in his memory! Suddenly he remembered his modest companion, remembered her timid devotion. Longing rose in him. "Debina! Debina!"

"Where is she?" asked Perri.

Tambo sighed. "I wish I knew!"

Perri sat leaning on her beautiful flag, holding both forepaws against her fluffy white breast. She sighed too. "Yes, everything good comes to an end some time. . . . Farewell, Tambo!" and she sped like a red streak toward the treetop.

Tambo could not fall asleep for a long time. "Debina," he thought. "Debina!" That he could have forgotten this name! That this lovely memory could have slipped away from him! He repeated Perri's observation: "Everything good comes to an end some time."

He could not remember how the end had come

about. How? And when? No matter how he pondered, no details came to him.

Had Debina deserted him? *She?* She who was so faithful and devoted; so patient, so unselfish? Impossible!

Then—had he run away from her? He? He remembered how panicky fright had once driven him away from her while she slept, and how she had searched for him, and found him.

No, he couldn't have deserted her. She would have followed him. She wouldn't have rested till she was near him again.

Or had some misfortune come to her?

Tambo's thoughts became confused. He slept fitfully, dreamed wildly, started up, left his bed even before gloaming.

"Debina, Debina!"

He grasped at the name which Perri had brought back to him.

He had never ranged so swiftly as on this moonlit night, had never grazed so sparsely, so hastily. Whenever he saw a doe he thought it was Debina. He stormed toward her, but when he saw that she was a stranger, and indifferent to him, he let her flee.

But there was one who did not flee when he ran up to her. An old one. She awaited his fierce approach placidly.

"Do you want something?" she asked. Her tone seemed sarcastic.

"Nothing of you," he answered gruffly and started to turn away.

"You thought I was someone else, Tambo."

"That's none of your business," he grumbled.

"Tambo, I know whom you're seeking."

In a flash he turned back.

"Your old friend, your Debina. Your *former* Debina." Now the irony sounded open.

He asked quickly, "Where is she?"

"I can tell you that too, Tambo. But it won't help you."

"Where? Where? Where?"

She described a certain part of the forest in exact

detail. Without thanks Tambo rushed away. And indeed, in a little glade he found Debina peacefully grazing. She looked up as he darted toward her.

"Debina!" he cried excitedly. "Debina!"

"Greetings," she said without emotion.

"Don't you know me?"

"Yes, I do. Tambo."

"Come with me," he begged eagerly. "I'm so happy to find you again. Come! We lost each other."

"Yes, Tambo, we lost each other." She spoke soberly.

"But don't think of that now," he implored. "Just come back to me. Our companionship was so beautiful."

"Yes, it was, Tambo. Beautiful . . ."

"It can be so again."

"Never, Tambo, never again."

"Because of someone else?" He flared up proudly.

She smiled gently. "Because of your child which will soon be born."

"My—my child?" he stammered.

"Yes, your child, Tambo. If it's a doe, I hope she'll be wiser than I was."

"Oh, Debina, no one could be so wise as you."

Calmly, she continued: "If it should be a male—then I want to see that he becomes as powerful as you. But he must never lose his dignity as his father lost his."

Hurt and ashamed, Tambo bowed his high-crowned head. "You're unjust, Debina! Unfair!"

Quietly, and this time without grief, she said, "Farewell, Tambo."

The word of parting struck his heart like a blow. He stayed rigid. A queer cloudiness swam before his eyes, so that he did not really see Debina's departure.

When he peered around finally, he found himself alone. He felt sad, incapable of decision. Without a goal, he wandered through the moonlit night. Now he cursed Perri. Why had the squirrel awakened his memory? What for? He had already forgotten Debina, had been almost happy again. . . . No, that wasn't true. He had not been happy the whole long time. Something had been wrong with him. What? Yes, what?

At first he had thought it was his bald head that was torturing him. His bald head! What a little thing indeed compared with the real cause. Yes, and now that was over. He could not count now upon her devotion to him alone.

But he did not know what his fault had been. He had lost his dignity, she had said. He didn't understand. He thought her unjust, but he mourned her bitterly.

Now the old doe came across his path.

"Don't grieve so, Tambo," she told him. "You're just learning a lesson of life. You will come to accept it. This is not serious. It's only in age that the really serious things come. Then you'll think how unimportant this was. It will seem distant and strange, as if it has never been."

But Tambo barely heard her and what he did hear he hardly comprehended.

Chapter 24

MARTIN HAD BEEN RIDING Devil on the wide forest road. But, as he rode without spur or whip, he had been unable to bring the usually prancing stallion to a gallop. Devil had always been willing, gay, even capricious. But throughout the winter his fiery temper had subsided and now, in the midst of beautiful spring, he was dull and ill-humored.

Martin rode him at a listless pace. Peter came forward to help Martin down and to unsaddle the stallion.

"There's some sort of change going on in this horse," the hunchback remarked as he dismounted clumsily.

"What do you mean, sir?" Peter asked.

"I can't explain it exactly. He's developed a lazy streak. And he's losing weight."

"Losing a little weight can hardly hurt him." Peter grinned.

As the two men left the stable together, Martin said worriedly, "I hope he hasn't the same illness poor Manni had—whatever it was."

"He's dissatisfied with you," Witch admonished the stallion.

"*Let* Him be, for all I care," Devil snorted.

"Don't let go of yourself," mooed Lisa. "It's not wise."

"Since when have I been wise?"

"You have enough wisdom to know what you owe Him," said Witch.

"Do I owe it to Him to be in good humor when I'm sad?"

Lisa spoke very gently. "You must stop grieving over Gray."

"Just look at me." Witch came to Lisa's support. "Have I lost my calm? I'm terribly unhappy about Gray. But sometimes I can be in quite a happy mood."

"Good girl," the cow praised her. "I was very fond of Gray. I mourn him, yet I'm usually in a good humor too."

"It's easy enough for you," answered Devil. "You didn't murder him."

"What a thing to say!" Lisa was indignant.

"But you didn't murder him either," Witch argued.

"Well, let's say killed. I killed my poor friend."

"No!" Witch cried out.

"Oh, you didn't!" Lisa exclaimed.

"You want to console me. Thank you." Devil spoke slowly. "But no matter how you turn and twist it, I'm still to blame for Gray's death."

The calf said in a grown-up tone, "It was an unfortunate accident."

A long silence.

Since Manni's passing, the stable company had not really enjoyed life. They had lost their confidence with the departure of the donkey, the happy-natured fellow who knew how to smooth over everything untoward, how to get around all difficulties. Now the daily round became dreary and forlorn.

Suddenly, to their vast astonishment, Peter brought in a new donkey, answering to the name of Raggo.

They greeted their new companion in friendliest fashion.

Raggo, however, was young, stupid and brash. By no means so easily satisfied as Manni, he wanted a stall all to himself.

"Get out, old thing!" he demanded of Witch. "That place is for me."

"You're mistaken, little one," Witch answered politely. "I've always lived here."

"I never make a mistake," snorted the donkey. "So, you've always lived here, eh? Bah! You're bragging."

"No," Devil mixed in. "She *has* always lived here."

"Did I ask you, old dopey-head? Speak when you're spoken to!"

The stallion was too surprised to answer.

Lisa, however, grumbled threateningly, "You'd better behave yourself, infant."

"Since when did I get to be your infant?" the donkey mocked.

"Not mine, Heaven forbid!" mooed Lisa. "But I advise you, don't get so fresh, infant."

The donkey went on sarcastically: "There's nothing I need more than your advice, you old milk-idiot!"

"Don't yap so," the stallion broke out. "We dislike such vulgarity."

"I don't give a hang what you like or dislike."

"If you're going to live with us, you must do as we do. Otherwise—"

"Otherwise?" the donkey threw in challengingly.

"We'll attend to you, infant!" The stallion showed a trace of his old fire.

"Well, you won't be done with me till you tell me where my predecessor used to live."

"Your predecessor," the stallion told him reverently, "was modest. He didn't ask a place for himself. He slept wherever he happened to be."

"Then he was plain dumb," laughed the donkey, "a moron."

"Not a word against Gray!" stamped the stallion.

"Yes, it's an outrage to criticize Gray!" Witch cried.

And Lisa mooed, "Just you dare, little one—just you dare criticize Gray. We'll throw you out!"

"Listen," said the stallion solemnly. "Gray, who was here before you, was wiser than all the rest of us put together."

"That doesn't mean much," the donkey threw in.

"Anyway," the stallion went on, "he had far more sense than you."

"And was more agreeable," said Witch.

"And much, much kinder," Lisa added.

"We all loved him," Witch explained softly.

The stallion sighed, "I wish he were still alive."

"You're all making yourselves ridiculous, raving over the dead."

"Out with you!" Lisa roared.

"You're old and silly—the whole kit and boodle of you," the donkey mocked.

The calf leaped forward. "Am *I* old?"

"No, not old," laughed the donkey, "but idiotic."

With lowered head the young calf attacked him. Raggo turned quickly and kicked out his hind legs.

But Lisa was already between them. "Aha, you fresh brat! There . . . !" She pushed her massive head into the donkey's flank. He staggered. "Get out!"

Witch gave the young donkey another push. "Yes, get out, you miserable little wretch!"

"Now! *Now*, Fiery One!" the cow urged the stallion. "*Now* let yourself go!"

"We've had enough of this asinine oaf!" cried Witch.

The donkey could not defend himself against the joint attack. He was hemmed in so that he could not kick and was soon weak from the buffeting they gave him. His punishers stood aside and he fled through the swinging door into the open.

Only slightly subdued, he stood outside and brayed at the top of his lungs.

Martin and Peter ran out of the house. The donkey brayed again pitifully. Martin stroked his head while Peter patted his flank.

"Go back into the stable," Martin urged him, and led

him inside. Emboldened by his bodyguard, he stepped like a conqueror straight into the mare's stall.

"Get away from me!" growled Witch.

"I won't!" replied the donkey, impudent again. "*You* get away!"

"I'll show you!" Witch threatened.

Martin and Peter left the stable, and the donkey did not wait for the mare's flailing hoof. Discreetly he slipped out of the stall and kept quiet.

Things were somewhat better after that day, but Raggo could never control his loose tongue. There was always quarreling in the stable, and he always had the worst of it. Sometimes he was driven out through the swinging door. His braying availed him little now, for Martin and Peter didn't come to his aid again. They knew the others' peaceable natures, knew the donkey was chiefly to blame, and hoped he'd be educated.

One thing they did not know was that the diversion of the new donkey's wrangling slowly freed the stallion from his brooding over Manni. None of the human beings had an inkling of how much the impudent young newcomer disturbed the stable inmates by the rows he was constantly provoking. Nor did they dream how much he refreshed them at the same time. Nor, in fact, did the stallion, the cow and the mare themselves realize it.

They believed that they hated the young whipper-snapper. They didn't notice that as a matter of strict truth they gradually began to like him very much.

Chapter 25

SPRING FLOWERED INTO SUMMER. Hot days warmed the forest floor, drying up the little puddles and the damp places. The brook became a brooklet, a tiny trickle, and then its bed dried up completely.

The roebucks shed their horns earlier than usual, and proudly, exuberantly, paraded in their beautiful red coats.

Again Genina walked with two fawns, a male and a female, substitutes for Loso and Mena. The pelt of both was still sprinkled with the white specks of first youth.

Loso, seeing Genina at a distance, said curtly, "Greetings," and quickly continued on his way. Genina did not attempt to answer him. A few months, even a few weeks, earlier, Loso's behavior would have hurt her very much. But now Loso's attitude was a matter of indifference to her. "He's young and giddy," she reflected indulgently.

Tender and happy, she looked at her new twins. "Nerba, Rambano," she whispered, "come closer to me." The little ones willingly obeyed their mother's call. "I love you terribly," said Genina very softly, "I love you both with all my heart!"

Rambano awkwardly tried a small leap of joy, and staggered on spread-out legs. "I love you too, mother!" he piped.

"So do I! I'll always love you, mother! Always!" Nerba pressed against Genina's side.

"We'll love you as long as we live, mother," Rambano promised. "All our lives. Only you!"

Genina should have known better. She might have

remembered Mena and Loso. Yet she had learned nothing from the way her lost first twins had treated her. She believed her new children's sweet promises and was quite happy.

A sharp, evil odor brought sudden terror into her contentment.

The fox!

"Stay close to me, children!" she warned. "Danger!"

The little ones too had caught the scent of the fox. Fearfully they trembled behind their mother.

Genina awaited the robber with determination. She would fight! Even if she had to die, the red killer would not get her children. But she would not die! A great anger streamed through the gentle Genina, a high, flaming, angry courage.

The fox slunk into view. When he saw the mother ready for battle, he hesitated.

At once Genina attacked him with flailing, drumming forelegs.

He ducked and parried, awaiting a favorable chance.

But Genina was lucky. She caught the hated enemy

square on the nose several times in lightning succession. With a yelp of pain he cowered away. Blood dripped from his snout.

Genina's heart beat to suffocation. Triumphantly she lifted her head. The children were saved! The red murderer would never dare come near them again.

"Be careful!" she told the little ones. "Don't leave my side. There are many other dangers!"

"We'll stay with you, mother," Rambano assured her.

"We never want to be without you, mother," said Nerba.

"That's my sweet little girl," Genina said, and regained her composure.

The twins danced clumsily around her.

Arilla joined them. "Greetings!" Her tone was friendly.

But Genina responded coolly, "Greetings!"

Arilla began the conversation with some embarrassment. "You have children again?"

"Can't you see for yourself?"

"Oh, yes! And two, at that."

"I always have two." Genina was proud.

"And I am still alone."

"Haven't you ever had children?" The mother roe peered at her curiously.

"No, never, Genina."

"You're unfortunate, Arilla." A kind of smug sympathy stirred in Genina.

Arilla laughed a little uncertainly. "Unfortunate? Not exactly . . ."

"But you were just complaining—"

"Oh, not really complaining. Whenever I see children with their mothers, as I see these with you, then at first I feel sorry I have none. Yet—"

"Arilla, what are you trying to say?"

"Well, only that I console myself—"

"How?"

Arilla was gaining confidence. "Since you ask me— well, *you*, with your experience, ought to know. What does one have, after all, from children? A little joy at the beginning? Yes, possibly. I admit it. Yet later nothing but fear and worry. Care. Heartache. The little ones slip away from you, and finally they actually leave you. What's the sense of the whole matter? What's it all for? A mother is always the fool of her children!"

Somewhere inside Genina there was a small sore spot; somewhere she sensed a breath of truth in Arilla's words. But her uneasiness passed quickly. "*You* can't talk about it, Arilla," she said shortly. "You don't know anything about it."

"Oh, yes I do," Arilla insisted petulantly.

"You haven't the *faintest* idea," Genina repeated with emphasis. "Remember, I told you once before that we two are badly suited for each other's company?" She turned away. "Come, children!"

Without further words she hurried off, her slim legs lifting proudly, the little ones dancing merrily by her side.

Arilla stared after her and muttered, "Blind, stupid thing!"

Genina wandered along the trail of the roes, coming presently to where Perri sat on a hazel bush cracking nuts.

"Greetings!" the squirrel called.

But before Genina could answer, Perri burst out admiringly: "What beautiful children! The darlings! You must be very happy, aren't you?"

"Indeed I am," Genina replied.

"You deserve it, my dear," said Perri and continued eagerly: "I must tell you something! Just a moment ago I saw that ruddy rascal. He must have got a fine blow on the nose from somebody."

Genina straightened up. "From me."

"Oh, wonderful!" rejoiced Perri. "Good for you! He was sneaking away, thoroughly licked! Aren't you brave! I'll tell this story everywhere!"

"Please do," Genina encouraged her. "Let all the robbers beware of attacking *my* children."

"They'll beware, all right!" Perri leaped to spread the tale.

Chapter 26

HIDDEN IN A NARROW HOLLOW thickly screened by bushes and shadowed by tall old oaks, Debina brought Tambo's baby into the world—a male.

With joyous excitement she washed her firstborn, carefully coaxed him to walk, delighted in his strong little body.

Knowledge was revealed to her of which she had never before dreamed. All of a sudden she knew everything; one moment she believed she had always known, then again that her wisdom stemmed from her little son, that all her knowledge had come into the world with him.

She decided to stay in her covert for a few days.

A finch happened to alight in the branches of an elderbush. He sang his glad verse over and over again. Debina listened to him and imagined his song to be a welcome to her little son, a tribute to herself. "Thank you, my good friend," she whispered to the finch. "It's nice of you to greet us."

As a matter of fact, the finch had given no heed to either Debina or her young one. Yet her thanks flattered him. This young queen of the forest was so gracious, and spoke so warmly. He remembered the courtesy that the situation called for.

"It's a great honor for me," he peeped, "that you notice me—a dwarf."

"You're a wonderful singer," Debina answered. "I'll never forget your exultant song."

Immediately the finch fluted his melody three or four times in succession, now truly for the honor of the queen and the tiny prince.

"Do you hear, my son?" Debina whispered. "Do you hear? The forest greets you! Life celebrates your coming!"

The fawn swayed insecurely on his thin legs.

"That's right," Debina encouraged. "Stout heart and sturdy legs, my child, and soon you'll leap and run!"

The finch spread his wings and flew away.

"Oh, now the singer is gone," Debina exclaimed. "Maybe you scared him away."

The finch, however, had flown away because the squirrel had dashed down from the treetops.

Perri rocked on the swinging seat of an oak limb and looked down at Debina.

"So here is where you are?" Perri laughed. "Greetings! I've been looking for you."

"Greetings," said Debina softly.

"I wish you luck. What a splendid prince you have!"

"You like my son?"

"I should say so! He's beautiful!"

"I've had him only a few hours."

"Is this your first baby?"

"Yes, my first."

Perri moved along the branch. "Well, I'll bear the news to the proud father."

"No, no, please! *Promise* me, Perri–not a word to Tambo!"

"Why not?" Perri was amazed. "Debina, I don't understand you! Tambo *is* the father, isn't he?"

"Of course Tambo is the father!"

"Well, then, why keep it secret from him?"

"Why–" Debina grew confused. "I can't explain it to you. . . . At least not so you'd understand. But don't tell him. Please . . ."

"All right, I'll keep quiet." The gossiping squirrel was disappointed. "But you're extraordinary, Debina. Farewell." Like red lightning, Perri rushed up to the treetop.

Left alone, Debina whispered to her young one, "*You'll* be my Tambo. My pride! My joy! Whether I'll live to see the time when you're a mighty ruler like your father–I don't know. I hardly believe I will. Yet one gift you shall have from me, your mother. Majestic dignity–that will be yours. You'll never forget who you are, what rank you have."

Little Tambo stood swaying helplessly. To him the eager whispering of his mother sounded like a dull roar. He understood nothing of what she said.

Now the magpie came whirring in and took a seat on a bush. "Perri told me about your prince," she began.

Debina nodded, a little worried at how quick the news was spreading.

"You're not exactly cordial, Debina."

"Oh, I'm sorry—"

"That's all right." The magpie was easily mollified. "I'm not angry."

"You have no reason to be."

"I like your son, Debina."

"I'm glad you do."

"When will you take him out?"

"Not very soon."

"Don't be foolish, Debina!"

"What do you mean?"

"I mean—after all—you can't hide your prince, you know."

"I don't want to do that. But for a few more days, I want to have him all to myself."

"But nobody will take him away from you."

Debina stiffened. "I wouldn't let anyone do that!"

"Well then? The prince must go out into the forest."

"But only a few days–"

"He'll be weak if he doesn't move around. He must walk so that he can leap and run."

"You're right. Oh yes, I–I know you're right. I'll take him out tomorrow."

"Good! You'll have great success with him."

"I hope so."

"And don't worry about Tambo."

"What makes you say that?" Debina felt her heart beat violently. Her ears jerked in alarm.

"Well, Perri told me you don't want him to know. But it's unnecessary."

"Unnecessary?"

"Tambo's not going to concern himself with his son."

Debina began to tremble with a new and strange emotion. "Nor with me?"

"Nor with you, Debina."

"I–I doubt that!"

The magpie chuckled harshly. "Well then, you'll find out. He's too self-centered to care for anyone but himself."

"Then—" Debina's soft voice quivered—"then he's changed greatly."

"Not at all! After you left him he became again what he was before. A strutting coxcomb."

"That's not so!" Debina defended Tambo hotly. "If it were, the whole forest wouldn't pay him such respect!"

"Respect? They all fear him for his strength. Fear! That's all!" The magpie whirred off.

The day inched onward. The rays of the sun shimmered singly through the foliage roof into the twilit covert. Debina was tired. She slept with the fawn pressed tightly to her. The little one too sank into a deep baby sleep.

Debina awakened when the moon hung full in the sky.

"Get up, little Tambo," she roused the fawn. "Let's go out."

Slowly she led and slowly he followed on wobbly legs. She slipped through the brush, holding the way open for the little one. It was some time before the path became wider and the thicket vanished except for a few bushes. At length they arrived at a clump of young trees.

A few roes who were grazing about jerked their heads up and fled at sight of the hind. *"Ba-uh!"* they cried. *"Ba-uh!"* over and over again. *"Ba-uh!"*

Little Tambo hung back. "Mother, what's that?" his wee voice piped, thrilling Debina.

"Our relatives, darling."

"Why did they run away, mother?"

"We deer would be glad to know that ourselves, my child."

From a distance came: *"Ba-uh! Ba-uh!"*

"Mother, why do they cry so loud?"

"Because they're frightened, precious."

"Why are they frightened?"

"Because they saw us so suddenly."

"Are we ugly, mother?"

"No, we're very beautiful. You especially, my dear."

"Then why, mother?"

"They think we're dangerous. They're afraid of us."

"But why are they afraid of us? Do we hurt them?"

"We don't hurt anyone, child."

"But then why–?"

"I don't know, darling. No deer understands it. But it cannot be changed."

"Why?"

"I can't explain it, son."

"Mother–"

"Yes?"

"Are they all afraid of us–*all* of them?"

"No, only some, here and there."

"Who, mother?"

"Who what, darling?"

"Who is afraid of–of who?"

"Sometimes a hare or a pheasant is frightened of us if we take them unawares."

"What's a hare?"

"Look around! You'll see them yourself. Just keep your eyes open."

They came to the edge of the wood. A meadow stretched away before them.

"Oh, I want to go there!" cried the little fawn.

"No, no!" His mother blocked his way. "First I must make sure no danger threatens."

"What's danger, mother?"

"Something that may hurt you. There are many

kinds of danger. We must be very cautious! Remember, my child, as long as you're with me you may never—understand now!—never go out into open space before I do. You must always wait until I say you may."

Debina then sniffed very carefully, found the air clear and stepped out. Behind her, obediently, came little Tambo.

By now he had a firmer step and as he came into the meadow he took his first leap.

"Good for you, son!" his mother praised him.

Some roes grazing in the meadow scattered. From all sides sounded their frightened cry. *"Ba-uh! Ba-uh!"*

Little Tambo laughed. "Now I know what that is!"

A hare sat up before him, both ears erect. Little Tambo jumped back to stare at the small fellow who said, "It's only I, my lad. Your friend the hare."

Quickly little Tambo responded, "Greetings, friend hare!"

"A handsome child you have, Debina," the hare said respectfully. "Good manners, too!"

A few other hares ran to join them. "What a beautiful prince," they said. "He has dignity already. Debina, our congratulations!"

Mother and son continued their way happily. Soon they had crossed the meadow. "The hares are nice," little Tambo piped.

He stayed behind his mother as she entered the thicket where high trees obscured the moonlight.

"Greetings!" called the gray owl. "A charming child you have there, Debina."

"I'm glad you like my son," said Debina. She was never tired of compliments for him, never tired of acknowledging them.

Little Tambo looked up toward the owl admiringly. This bird with feathered ears and shining eyes fascinated him. Timidly he ventured another "Greetings."

The owl hooted, "Greetings, young prince." She turned to Debina. "Your son is polite. I approve of him!" She spread her wings and floated away. "Till we meet again!" she called back.

Little Tambo stared after her. "Mother," he asked, "she looks wise. Is she?"

"She's very wise," Debina said. "No one in all the forest has such wisdom as the owl."

"Owl," repeated the fawn. "Owl . . . owl . . . that's a funny name."

"Yes," Debina answered absently. "No! No, of course it isn't! It's a very fine name. And you should be proud that she praised you so highly!"

They wandered deeper into the forest. Little Tambo laughed and frolicked. Debina was elated by the ovation given her child.

A sharp evil scent suddenly filled her nose. She stopped and called, "Come close to me, little Tambo!" She knew that smell. The fox!

Little Tambo too caught the bad odor and ran to his mother, his thin legs trembling.

"Greetings, Debina," barked the fox softly. "Don't be afraid."

"I'm not afraid of you, Red," Debina told him haughtily. Then she added, "Greetings."

"So you greet me again." The fox leered. "I've never forgotten that you did so once before. And I never will."

"What do you want of me now?" Debina preserved her haughtiness.

"Nothing. Except to wish you luck with your delightful child."

"Many thanks, Red."

"You don't call me robber or murderer anymore."

"No, not anymore."

"You *are* nice, Debina."

"Never mind that, Red."

Wishful drops dribbled from the fox's jaws. "Your son is appetizing. He'd be a fine meal for me. But be calm, I'll spare him."

"I'm calm because you can't do anything to him! Not even if you wanted to!"

"So *you* think. I'm very hungry, Debina." The saliva fairly dripped from his fangs. "So far I have only mice in my stomach."

"Go, Red! Fetch yourself five or six more mice."

He burst out, "I'd attack anybody else. But not you or yours!"

"You're right. I'd kill you without mercy."

"Perhaps it would be an interesting struggle!" the fox said slyly.

"Be off now, Red, quickly." Debina was breathing hard. "We have nothing more to say to each other. Farewell!"

Slinking off, he said over his shoulder, "Thank you for the greeting and farewell." And as if removing himself from temptation, he loped away.

Little Tambo stood quaking. "That's 'danger'—isn't it, mother?"

"Yes, my child, one of our many dangers. But grow big and strong and there's hardly any danger you'll ever need to fear."

Putting aside all worry, Debina delighted in little Tambo, in his growing agility and queer clumsy grace, in the obedience he showed despite his lively temperament.

A few strong stags passed her and her son, who looked at these apparitions in wonder. While the high-crowned Kings nodded in friendly fashion to the little one, Debina felt a certain premonition.

Now King Tambo stepped along, overpowering with the size and splendor of his crown.

Debina halted, waiting, breathless. Would he address her? Would he greet his son? For a moment she hoped so and felt inclined to permit his advances as the beginning of new friendship—an enduring companionship.

The majestic figure came closer, very close.

Debina stepped into his path as if by accident, and stopped, pretending to be surprised. Tambo could not help but see her and the little one. Yet he did not give her a single glance! He looked neither at her nor at his son. Like a complete stranger he passed them by, regal, indifferent, unapproachable.

Debina felt cold and suddenly hostile. The magpie's words spoke in her. *Strutting coxcomb!...*

"Come!" she bade the youngster, who was staring fascinated after Tambo. She would not say to her fawn, "That is your father."

She had her son ... at least she had her son. He was all that mattered now. *He* would not, must not, could not disappoint her....

Chapter 27

EEP DARKNESS PREVAILED. NO moon stood in the heavens and the stars were invisible behind the clouds. Yet the fox was still seeking prey.

Mad hunger plagued him. For he had made not a single catch; not a rabbit, not even a mouse. His hunger had grown to violent cramps which drove the unsuccessful robber to desperation.

A hare rose suddenly before him and fled. Filled with hatred the fox stared after him, but did not feel strong enough to catch up with the fugitive, or even to ambush him by a short cut.

Then a mouse came into his path, and he crushed it and swallowed it with lightning speed. Yet the tiny bite only made his pangs the sharper. Hoarse barking ripped from his throat.

"Am I so clumsy? Am I too dumb to satisfy my appetite? Or am I having extra bad luck? I missed the pheasants too."

Longingly he looked up into the trees. He could see dark motionless clumps—pheasants asleep, each with his head tucked under a wing.

What a delicious feast, a pheasant like that! The fox's mouth watered. "I wish I knew how to climb. Then I'd be full in a trice."

Dreamily he dragged himself farther along. At last he sat on his haunches to rest, dull, tired, starving.

Up in a treetop, suddenly, he heard a short choking cluck and the panicky beating of wings. Electrified, the fox leaped to the tree. His every nerve vibrated with newly awakened strength; he was ready for battle. Just let whoever was killing that pheasant bring it down to the ground and he'd never enjoy his booty! The fox would see to that!

He felt so strong through his bitter need that he was sure he could conquer even the fiercest enemy. Yes, if he could kill this lucky pheasant-catcher, instead of just putting him to flight, he'd have a double meal! His fasting would be over for a long time!

The throttled squawks and the wild flapping in the tree had grown feeble. Feverishly the fox lurked about to see if the invisible robber would come down. It would be terrible if he were to do all his feasting up in the tree! But no, that was never done right on the scene, the fox knew. If only a few paces away, a quiet place must be found. At night, only the owl gobbled her food in the trees. And in the daytime, the hawk. However, the owl never attacked pheasants, and at night the hawk was sleeping. So this killer couldn't be one of those.

Tense, ever more confident, more insane with greed and the desire to fight, the fox waited. It was no more than a few moments, but it seemed to him an eternity.

In the branches, a new rustling sounded. Slowly someone climbed down, very slowly, with the dead pheasant, a heavy load. Now the invisible robber stopped on a branch to rest.

Impatiently the fox panted with hanging tongue.

A thud! *The pheasant fell to the ground.*

Had it slipped from the stranger's grasp or had he thrown it down? No matter! Like lightning the fox leaped to seize the fallen prey.

And as quickly Shah the Persian tomcat landed on the ground and rushed for his booty.

The fox snarled, baring his teeth. He had never seen the tomcat before, did not know his kind, and sized him up for a weakling. "He won't fight," he told himself, "and if he does, I'll settle him in no time!"

Bravely, however, with angry hissing, the tomcat showed himself ready to attack. Against his natural enemy, here in the forest, the gentle pet of the barnyard became a thing of fury.

"Give me my prey!" he demanded fiercely. "Give me my property, you red ruffian!"

"Nothing here is your property," rumbled the fox. "Who *are* you, anyway?"

"I'll show you who I am, you highjacker!" the tomcat yowled in rage.

"You don't live in the forest!" yapped the fox. "You've got no right here!" He crouched to attack.

The tomcat hit at his eyes with quick sharp claws.

Caught by surprise, the fox jerked back just in time. The claws had cut him on the forehead, had almost cost him an eye. It wasn't so simple as he thought to deal with this enemy!

The big teeth in the fox's long jaw planted respect in Shah too.

Growling and snarling, they crouched opposite each other, both taking stock. It was the Persian again who reached the first conclusion.

He sprang on the fox's back, and delivered a drum-fire of blows against the red robber's head and eyes. The fox threw himself backward, his eyelids tightly closed; he rid himself of the attacker and snapped at him wildly. He reached for Shah's throat, grimly trying to bite it through. But the nimble tomcat knew how to avoid him and his fangs. Suddenly the fox caught the Persian's ear. His teeth held tight, tearing. The tomcat gave a howl of pain and wrenched loose.

More than the tip of the ear stayed in the fox's mouth. He swallowed it quickly, and tried to jump on the tomcat. But Shah slipped from under his paws.

The great gray owl floated soundlessly over the two embattled enemies and looked at them curiously. "What's going on down there?" She lighted on a branch.

The fox shouted angrily, "This stranger here won't leave me the pheasant he killed!"

"Stranger?" gurgled the owl. "This fellow's no stranger to me."

"You know him?"

"I know him very well. He's not doing this out of hunger. He kills like his two-legged masters—from sheer wantonness."

"When I'm so hungry!" the fox yowled.

"Take care of your eyes!" the owl cried. "He's just as evil as those two-legged traitors he lives with. They set a burning trap for me! He's just as dangerous!"

"Do you live with Him?" the fox snapped.

"None of your business!" Shah spat back.

"See here," the owl joined in, "after all, you don't have to come up here to our place and play robber!"

"I do whatever I want!" the tomcat snarled.

The owl's curved beak clacked. "Don't be fresh or you'll get something from me too—understand!" She floated down almost to the ground and glared at the Persian with huge fiery eyes.

. The tomcat ducked back, frightened.

The owl told the fox, "This glutton lives an easy life with those two-legged fools. They love him. They give him sweet milk to drink. They feed him so full he can't eat it all. He has a soft warm bedding place, and can do anything he wants. The two-legged idiots don't know he still comes up here. You're shameless!" she raged at the tomcat. "You'll have a lot of trouble if you think you can do whatever you want *here*. Run back to Him before you're sorry!"

"I want my property first!" snarled the tomcat.

"Nothing here is your property," the owl mocked. "Your life belongs to you, nothing else. Take that and get out. Or else you'll lose it as you lost your ear!"

The fox plunged to still his hunger on the pheasant. He tore at the flesh of the fat bird, swallowing greedily.

"Must I watch this calmly?" the tomcat yelled and sprang again on the fox's back. Foaming, the fox turned his neck to get at the other's throat. The Persian somersaulted, grabbed for the torn pheasant and would have fled.

But the owl, suddenly wanting a share of the loot, prevented him. Her wings beat around his head, her sharp claws stabbed at his throat and face like daggers.

Shah tried to defend himself, to fight and resist. But his paws hit empty air. Blinded by the owl's wings, he dropped the pheasant.

"*Grab!*" the owl cried to the fox.

He misunderstood her on purpose and seized the pheasant.

"I mean grab the black thief!" the owl shrieked indignantly. "Grab him, choke him!"

The tomcat used this moment to jump free, for he was wounded and felt the nearness of death. Maddened by pain he ran wildly, as desperately as his feet would carry him, toward the valley. Behind him loped the fox. Above him floated the owl. To escape the owl he slipped into the thick underbrush.

The fox followed him, egged on by the owl and now hoping to fulfill his dream of killing and eating his enemy.

In the thicket, branches and thorns scraped Shah's raw wounds. That slowed him down. He felt dull and sensed the fox catching up. He tried to reach the open stretch and, collecting his last strength, fled down the hill to the Lodge garden.

Closer above him floated the owl. She was still following him when he reached the garden fence. There the fox had to stop. Wearily, he sneaked back to his pheasant.

The tomcat kept running right to the stable. The owl swooped down in vicious farewell. "Don't you ever dare show yourself in our forest again, you villain! Never again!" The Persian disappeared through the swinging door.

The owl flew back to the woods and found the fox enjoying the last of the pheasant. "Give me my share!" she said. "I helped you."

"I didn't need your help," snapped the fox.

"Don't be ungrateful, Red," the great owl warned. "We chased that rascal away together. He'll never come here again." She snatched and swallowed a piece of meat covered with feathers.

The fox growled, "If you hadn't chased him away, I'd have killed him myself and would have still more to eat. So, as a matter of fact, you helped *him!*"

"No boasting, Red," the owl's beak clacked. "I've eaten only a little anyway, and you're full."

The fox had to admit that. He was no longer hungry and felt more good-natured.

The owl floated away. They were both satisfied, yet they did not exchange words of parting.

Chapter 28

W HEN THE TOMCAT BURST into the barn, Raggo the donkey was awake. "For land's sake, little one, what happened to you?" He loved to pass on to the tomcat the manner of the others toward himself.

The exhausted Persian was in a bad mood. "Shut up!"

"I'm sorry for you, little one. You're bleeding."

"Well, what of it? What do you care?"

"It's none of my business, of course, little one,"

retorted the donkey, "but I'm still sorry for you."

"Shut up, I said!" the tomcat snarled.

"And one of your ears is missing, you poor thing."

"Ear? Oh, yes, my ear. I bit it off myself. It annoyed me . . ."

"Bit it off yourself?" the donkey marveled. "I couldn't do that, and my ears are much longer."

"Yes, you have nice ears," the tomcat said hastily, ashamed of his stupid explanation.

"How'd you get those cuts on your neck and over your eyes? They're bleeding badly. All that from the owl?"

"What do you mean—from the owl? What do you know about the owl?" Shah paused in his smoothing of his ruffled fur.

"Well, I heard her scold you and forbid you the forest."

"Oh! . . . Well, don't tell the others about it," the tom-cat begged.

"The new Little Gray isn't the only one who knows," mooed Lisa unexpectedly. "The owl was loud enough."

The startled Persian limped over to her. "You heard too?"

"I certainly did," the cow rumbled. "And now that you're here—come on, be honest—who took your ear?"

Sullenly the tomcat's nose sank and he admitted: "The fox."

Raggo said, "I knew you couldn't have done it yourself!"

"Does it hurt very much?" Lisa asked.

"Not so much now."

Filled with curiosity, the donkey inquired, "It must have felt horrible to have it bitten off, didn't it?"

Shah just nodded.

Raggo wanted to know more. "Of course you ran away at once?"

The Persian's battle-scarred head jerked up. "No! That shows how little you know me."

Witch awoke. "What are you all talking about?"

Before she could get an answer, Devil stood beside her. "Look how this free and independent friend of ours is bleeding! His whole ear's gone!"

"Only half," contradicted the Persian.

"The whole thing!" the stallion reaffirmed. "You can't see it."

"But I can feel it!" said the tomcat, much irritated.

The stallion maintained his opinion. "Seeing is what counts."

"You think you know everything." The tomcat spat.

"And no one doubts that I do!"

"*I* doubt it." Shah resumed smoothing and cleaning his ruffled fur. "As far as I'm concerned, you're witless. I can see right through you."

"Not with those clawed-up eyes you can't," snorted the stallion.

Raggo declared, "It looks to me as if the owl and the fox had got the best of you."

"And serves you right!" the stallion muttered with satisfaction. "Why did you run up to the forest secretly? Why do you kill hares and pheasants? Does He let you go hungry?"

"Let him alone, Fiery One," Lisa begged softly. "He must be suffering great pain."

"Serves him right!" the stallion repeated stubbornly. "Playing robber will be beaten out of him yet! One day he'll be minus his other ear, and then they'll kill him. Good riddance if this murderer dies!" The stallion tossed his head.

The Persian cried out, "Murderer yourself! Cowardly murderer! Grass-eating murderer!"

In a flash they all turned on the tomcat.

"You're shameless!" Witch raged.

Lisa mooed indignantly. "You wanton meat-gobbler, you know very well the Fiery One didn't want to kill his friend!"

The calf spoke up with his favorite line: "It was an unhappy accident."

The donkey had little idea what was meant. He made mental guesses which evoked dreadful images in his mind. For some time now he had suspected that Manni had been beaten to death by the stallion. That made him afraid of Devil and toned down his sauciness. He had grown more modest, more agreeable, at times even humble. And so a friendly harmony had prevailed in the stable.

Subdued by his unpopularity today, the tomcat fled to the feed box, where he sat defiantly with his back to the wall.

The donkey felt sorry for him, and began to excuse and even praise him. "You've got to admit he's spunky.

He's still got spirit, in spite of his pain. He's really sick and badly wounded."

"Well, we're not doing anything to him," Lisa mooed good-naturedly.

"None of us would think of hurting him," Witch declared.

The stallion said grudgingly, "I forgive the plucky little fellow."

"He did fight bravely against the owl and the fox, didn't he?" Raggo insisted.

"Oh yes, very bravely," Lisa agreed.

"The owl? Did he fight the owl too?" Witch was amazed.

The donkey recounted what he had heard when Shah had come running in.

"And I heard it, too," the cow bore witness.

"Fine!" the stallion exclaimed. "Good for the owl!"

"*Good* for her?" demanded the tomcat. "For her deceitful, brutal attack? For the wounds she gave me?"

"No, not for that," said the stallion. "But for telling you to keep out of the forest."

"I'll go again just the same, in spite of her!"

The stallion flew into a fit of his old anger. "You will not!"

"I will! I must revenge myself on the fox," the tomcat said.

"Yes, just think of it!" The donkey took Shah's part again. "He didn't flee after the fox bit off his ear. Instead—" He turned to the tomcat. "What *did* you do?"

"I attacked the red thief!" The Persian glowed with pride.

The donkey was proud too. "*Isn't* he a brave little fellow?"

The stallion pronounced his reluctant judgment. "These meat-eaters, these robbers, are all very brave. All of them."

"The fox," Lisa grumbled, "must be very dangerous."

"He is!" Devil agreed. "I don't know him—I never saw him—but I know he's very ferocious."

"Ferocious! Dangerous!" mocked the Persian. "He's just a thief! A miserable, greedy, craven thief."

"What did he steal from you?" Witch asked mildly.

"The pheasant I caught in a tree." Shah spat.

"Oh! . . . Well, you leave the pheasants in peace," the stallion cautioned him. "You can eat your fill here. He gives you enough."

"But nothing alive, nothing I catch myself."

"That's not so," Lisa contradicted. "There are lots of mice here."

"What's a mouse!" the tomcat retorted disdainfully.

"And rats," Witch added.

The Persian wiped his mouth with a paw. "Rats make me sick at my stomach. I only bite their necks. I wouldn't touch them otherwise."

The stallion said, "Just the same, it's something alive."

"But what's that compared with a pheasant?" demanded the tomcat. "The pheasant sleeps high in the trees. The fox can't get up there because he can't climb. No He can reach him without a thunder-stick. But *I* can get up there quickly—right into the tree. Softly I sneak very close. The pheasant doesn't wake up. A bite—and he's mine!"

The stallion shuddered. "Dreadful!"

The cow was speechless with horror.

"Awful!" the calf groaned.

Witch whirled. "I don't want to hear about it!"

The donkey stared at the Persian.

"*You* can't understand this, you grass-eaters." Shah felt very superior. "The hunt is ecstasy for which I gladly risk everything. But surely you can understand my fury when the fox stole my prey—*my* property—and tried to tell me I had no right to it! Oh, if that treacherous owl hadn't helped him, I'd have taken care of him all right!"

"Or he of you," Lisa observed.

Just then Babette entered the stable to milk the cow. At first she didn't notice the tomcat crouching by the feed box. The milk gushed into the pail in hot jets and spread sweet fragrance.

Attentively, as he did every morning, the donkey stood and watched.

Lisa was enjoying the pleasant relief that the emptying of her udder now gave her. Witch whispered across the stall partition to her, "When our two-legged friend sees him, he'll be in for it!"

"She won't see him," the stallion pointed out. "Little Gray is standing in the way on purpose."

"When she does see him," Witch whispered gloatingly, "he'll be punished. No milk!"

Lisa lifted her broad beautiful head. "You're wrong," she mooed, so loud that the others were frightened lest Babette understand her. "You're wrong. She'll pamper that scoundrel."

Babette said, "I'm finished already, brown Lisa. You're impatient today." She rose and picked up the full milk pail.

The donkey had to step aside to let Babette pass.

Now the Persian wanted to show his stable companions how much he remained in favor. Besides, he wanted to drink his milk. He was thirsty and longed for refreshment and for tenderness from the two-legged ones in whose goodness he had confidence. He gave a plaintive *miaow* and made as if to leap down off the feed box.

Babette saw him. "Yes, Shah! There you are! Come— *milk!*" she called. Then she noticed his wounds. She uttered a little cry. "For heaven's sake, what have they done to you? Who did it?"

She took hold of him gently. Even her tender touch made his wounds hurt again, most of all the deep ones the owl's claws had made on his back and throat. He gave a chattering mew of pain and drew away.

But Babette persisted carefully. "Come, darling," she soothed, "I won't hurt you. I only want to help you."

The tomcat crept into her arms, though her touch still hurt him.

"Oh, Shah, how terribly hurt you are! How you've bled—"

He chattered again at Babette's attempt to caress him.

"Your ear . . . !" Babette wailed. "Your beautiful ear!"

The Persian miaowed with pain. Then the sweet fragrance of the milk rose into his nostrils. His throat was dry. He ached for a refreshing drink and tried to get out of Babette's arms.

"Yes, yes, you can have your milk." She let him slip easily to the floor. "I'll give you anything you want."

She fetched the milk pail from Lisa's stall and filled the saucer which always stood ready for the Persian. "There, poor darling."

Eagerly the Persian lapped. The milk refreshed him and gave him new strength.

Babette bent over him. "Your neck! Your forehead! And that ear! How can we heal you?"

The tomcat had just finished when Peter entered the stable to feed the horses and the donkey.

"Look at Shah," Babette said.

Peter stooped and looked the wounds over. "There's not much to be done here," he said gravely.

"Is—is he done for?" quavered Babette.

"Practically," Peter said. "A shot would put him out of his misery."

"No!" Babette exclaimed. "No! No! I'll nurse him back to health!"

Soberly Peter said, "I'm afraid he has too many wounds."

"He must have had a wild fight with other tomcats, Peter."

Peter shook his head. "Not wounds like these. These come from fiercer enemies."

"From whom, for heaven's sake?"

"How should I know?"

"No matter who did it," Babette concluded, "in my care he'll get well again." She took up the milk pail and left the stable, Peter following.

Lisa mooed in disgust. "Well, what did I tell you? Are these two-legged fellows stupid or not?"

"They're good," snorted the stallion.

"They're good out of pure stupidity," argued Lisa.

"Then let's be glad they're stupid," was the opinion of Witch the mare, "if it means they help us."

"Pardon me," the donkey put in, "but *I* think they're very wise."

"Much wiser than you, at any rate." The cow dismissed him.

Devil snorted, "That's not saying much."

Chapter 29

THE WINTER DRAGGED ON. TWICE Martin and Peter rode the horses, followed by Raggo, to take feed to the forest—clover, chestnuts and turnips, which they scattered about for the wild animals. It pleased the horses and the donkey to crunch through the forest in the snow.

One day when the men had gone off in the thicket, the roes approached the barn animals timidly. Genina recognized them quickly. "Greetings! How are you?"

"Genina! We're very well, thank you," the stallion replied.

"And you?" Witch inquired.

"Oh, whenever we have hay and chestnuts, we do very well."

Witch looked at Genina's two children. "Are they still so small?" she asked in surprise.

Genina laughed. "Oh no, these are new ones."

"Wouldn't you like to visit us again?" Devil invited. "We'd be very pleased."

"Thank you, but it's not dangerous here now. I'd rather stay in the forest."

"We wish you'd come," Witch said with regret.

"This is a younger Gray," Genina observed. "Where's the old one?"

"He's not alive anymore," Witch whispered.

"Oh, how sad!" Genina bowed her head. "I liked him very much."

"But the new Little Gray has earned our friendship," Witch explained quickly.

"Is that so? He looks nice. I must go now. Farewell!"

And Genina departed with her fawns at her side while the other roes marveled at her boldness.

The second time the stable animals brought feed they met the bald-headed stags, who displayed less confidence than the roes and fled. The stallion quickly overtook one of them. "Why are you running away? You needn't be afraid. We won't do anything to you."

"We're not running away out of fear," countered the young stag. "We're fleeing out of shame." He took courage and stopped now to talk. Witch joined them.

"Why are you ashamed?" the stallion asked.

"Don't you see?—we're not wearing our crowns."

"Where are they?" Witch inquired with sympathy.

"Lost—shed," said the young stag.

"That's funny!" said the donkey, shaking his head.

"There's nothing funny about it." The young stag was good-natured. "Our little relatives are very shy. Do you know them?"

"Oh, yes," the stallion boasted. "A doe and her two fawns once lived with us for a whole winter."

"Growing the crown hurts, doesn't it?" Witch asked.

"Not at all. We feel happy. There's a pleasant itching and tickling we can feel through our whole bodies. Then when the crown is ripe and hard, we rub off the covering."

"Very interesting!" nodded the stallion. "It's nice of you to explain it to us."

"Very nice," Witch agreed. "Many thanks."

"Oh, we're glad to do it. Farewell!" In high galloping leaps the young stag hurried away.

The three—stallion, mare and donkey—looked after him.

"I think these free creatures are wonderful," said Witch. "They can always do whatever they want."

"Yes," the donkey agreed, "they're both wild and tame, timid and bold."

"I'm glad I stopped him." The stallion was full of self-satisfaction. "That's the first time we've been able to talk with our free brothers."

"I wouldn't care for that kind of freedom," the donkey declared. "If I were free, I wouldn't know what to do with myself. And it's too risky."

"I like to serve," the stallion admitted. "To serve and have plenty to eat is better than freedom."

"And more secure," Witch pointed out. "What a fine, safe, comfortable place our barn is!"

They trotted contentedly back to the stable, Martin riding the stallion and Peter the mare. Raggo loped behind alone.

After the snowy cold of the forest they welcomed the pleasant warmth of their home. The oats tasted better than usual.

"Did you have a good time?" mooed Lisa.

"Yes, but there's nothing better than our stable and our kind of life," said Devil, chewing oats.

Raggo went into a detailed description of their meeting with Genina and the young stag.

The cow listened with interest. "As soon as there's hot sun again out there," she announced, "I'll take a walk up into the forest myself."

Chapter 30

THE WINTER CONTINUED SEVERAL weeks more. Then a thawing wind swept over the icy earth from the south, breaking up the frost and melting the snow with its breath. Everywhere water dripped and splashed. The forest was flooded, the brook swelled to a mad torrent.

One day the wild geese streaked homeward toward the far north. Their flight proceeded as always. At the head flew the leader, the others following in two lines that formed a wedge. Their honking was a high shout of freedom. And they brought first news of the spring that was approaching hesitantly amid storms and rain squalls.

Scattered white flakes danced in the streams of rain splashing down, but they dissolved as soon as they touched the ground.

One morning the sun shone blindingly. With a chirping cry a blackbird lifted himself to the top of a leafless tree and there started his song of rejoicing. It was short at first, but as he repeated it evening and morning each day, it grew longer and more enchanting.

Sprouting foliage spread from tree to tree, from bush to bush and over the open ground.

Squirrels slipped out of their nests, rubbed their eyes, exercised up one branch and down the other, waved their saucy flags.

Like silver-gray balls of wool the newborn March hares played and nibbled at fresh grass and foliage.

For the fox the time of starving, of living only on mice, was past. He caught clumsy young hares, and also gobbled up a hare mother who fell before his attack. Pheasants, noisily beating their wings, fluttered to the ground from their sleeping-trees, announcing them-selves lustily with bursts of clucking. The fox ambushed them without trouble.

Another morning, and the forest was filled with the flight and the song of masses of birds returning from the south. The cuckoo called, timidly at first, with long pauses. The oriole swung from one treetop to another, never tired of repeating, "I am he-ere! I am ha-appy!" Swallows swooped through the air or industriously built their nests.

The birds who had stayed at home made a hubbub too.

The jay screeched disapproval. "What an uproar! Quiet!" But nobody paid any attention to him. The magpies chattered, asking everyone about their adven-tures. The titmice whispered busily in the underbrush. The woodpecker hammered on the tree trunks, drum-ming like mad and laughing metallically. The finches pealed their amusing strain. The robins simply sang.

Many roes appeared in the groves and meadows. Their young ones followed the example of the grownups and kept to themselves.

Whenever they met stags, they fled quickly as always.

From all sides came their frightened *Ba-uh!*—sometimes deep, sometimes thin and high.

Now the stags' crowns grew powerfully. Though they had not yet reached their full size, the covering made them seem huge.

From afar Debina saw Tambo. Her sharp eyes made her doubt that he would remain King this time. He had grown old, she saw. And she saw that his crown would not be so strong as usual. It was a sixteen-pointer, a mighty one among all the others. But Tambo would not be a ruling tyrant as before. She was certain of that. She felt sorry for him and would gladly have made up with him.

She looked at little Tambo happily gamboling around her.

He had the beginnings of tremendous horns. He would outdo his father. He would be king, more power-ful than Tambo had ever been; prouder, always remem-bering his dignity.

Debina knew that and was proud of her son.

Should she tell him now who his father was? Now? Debina couldn't make up her mind.

Chapter 31

THE NIGHT WAS DELICATELY touched by silver moonlight. Deep shadows lay in the bushes under the high trees.

The Persian tomcat had been cured by Babette's nursing through the winter months. And now there arose in him a new desire for adventure, a new craving for revenge.

He had almost forgotten the pain he had endured, though sometimes in his torn ear he thought he felt the fox's bite, sharp enough to make him cry out.

At such times Babette took him tenderly in her

arms, petted him and spoke to him soothingly. Shah purred and pressed against her. Though he did not understand her words, their tone calmed him.

Tonight his old longing to catch a pheasant drove him back to the forest. Quietly, cautiously, he slipped through the dark bush, avoiding the moonlit places as much as possible or else flashing quickly across them.

He pictured himself leaping from a tree onto the neck of the unsuspecting fox and getting his revenge quickly.

He hoped the great gray owl would not be there this time. It was not the fox, but the owl, that Shah feared most. But it was the fox he hated. Only after a knock-out battle, after fully enjoying his vengeance, he promised himself, would he fetch away the pheasant, his reward.

But there were flaws in this sly plan.

For it happened that the fox was accompanied by two young foxes already expert in mouse catching and hare killing. They were young, keen, fierce fellows, eager to kill and with clamoring appetites.

Before he saw them, Shah darted like a black streak across an open moonlit space.

Lightning-fast, the young foxes sprang after him. But they found nothing and turned back, puzzled. The old fox drew his forepaw to his body like a pointing dog and sniffed upward toward where the tomcat crouched half-hidden by the thin foliage of a tree.

Horrified, Shah stared down, hardly daring to believe his eyes. *Three* foxes! All he needed now to be quite lost was for the owl to come!

"So it's you, you dirty intruder?" shouted the fox. And the other two at his side yelped, "Dirty intruder!"

The tomcat spat his answer: "Yes, it's I, you cowardly thief!"

"Are you bringing me your other ear?"

"I've come to fetch your eyes!"

"Come down and try it!" the fox barked mockingly.

A silence fell. The Persian was pondering how to save himself. After all, there were no pheasants to be seen. He heard the fox's yap again.

"You won't learn your lesson, poacher, till you've had your throat slit!"

The cat let this threat too go without retort. Moving

stealthily, he slipped to the other side of the tree to reach the next one without returning to the ground. Up here, at least, it was safe. Not even the great gray owl could get at him if he stayed where the branches were thickest. At any rate, she'd be only one enemy.

The brave mood that had filled Shah before was disappearing. He jumped, and the dry, rotten branch of the next tree, a birch, broke under his weight. He almost plunged into the open jaws of the three foxes. The pulse beat in his ears with fright, making the old bite throb painfully. With a desperate effort he clung to the bark of the tree trunk, then climbed up furiously.

Down below the foxes moved to the foot of the birch. "We'll get you!" gloated the old fox. "We'll soon have you!"

Agilely, Shah sneaked farther, whipping from one tree to another and at last managing to leave the trailing foxes behind. But then he came to a clearing. He stopped in dismay. Should he risk it on the ground, or stick to the trees and make a wide detour of the clearing?

He didn't dare go down to the ground. It would be

his bitter end if those red robbers caught up with him! He chose the detour.

It proved to be long and difficult. But the tomcat was patient, for he hoped to confuse his pursuers.

Suddenly close behind him a cry shrilled.

Rigid with fright, Shah turned to see the little hoot owl measuring him with glowing eyes.

"Did I scare you?" the hoot owl asked.

The sight of an owl—even such a very small owl—broke the cat's proud spirit entirely. Shah didn't want to fight now. Terrified, he wanted only to escape.

Wistfully the hoot owl called, "Hello! I think you're nice!"

But the frantic Persian fled.

The sociable hoot owl floated after him. "Are you in a great hurry? Wait a minute! Let's have a little chat!"

Shah didn't answer. He leaped, scrambling and tumbling through the trees, thumped and scratched by the boughs. Finally he bounded to the ground and went springing like a hare, faster than he had ever run in his life. Behind him floated the little hoot owl, like some fearful spirit, it seemed to Shah, calling "Wait! Wait!"

But Shah didn't wait. On he bounced and bounded until at last he reached the familiar garden gate. Never had it looked so dear to him! Over it he sailed and—nearly overcome by a sense of safety—staggered on toward the barn.

"Whew, that was a close call!" he gasped, slipping thankfully through the stable door. "I'll never go to that murderous place again!" he vowed, shuddering. "*Really*, never again!"

Beyond the garden, the puzzled and disappointed little hoot owl floated back to the forest.

Chapter 32

N THE SPLENDID SPRING DAY after Shah's fateful night Martin the hunchback wandered through the forest. He was alone. When a grazing roe fled, or another stayed and looked at him with confidence, he smiled.

A stag leaped across his path. Martin stood without moving.

The stag stopped too, stared at the man calmly, then comfortably departed. Martin heard his steps through the thicket. Pleased, he continued on his way to his lookout platform. Just before he reached it, something rustled in the grass.

The fox!

Frightened, the red one stood still and stared at Martin.

"What a wise face," thought Martin, holding himself very still. "It's almost like the head of a good dog... but the expression isn't good. He looks as if he had a bad conscience."

The two were barely five paces apart. The fox seemed hypnotized by the benevolent look of these human eyes.

"Poor fellow," thought Martin, "you have a hard time in your world of freedom. I don't begrudge you the hare or the pheasant you capture."

The fox sneaked away, turning his head suspiciously again and again, until finally his watcher could no longer see him.

Martin climbed up to the platform, sat down and looked around. Like a thirsty man drinking, he drew air into his humped chest.

"Nowhere else," he said to himself, "can I breathe so

easily as up here. Nowhere else does my heart feel free."

His glance swept across the ocean of green treetops and over the plowed fields in the distance. He put his field glasses to his eyes, and searched the preserve he knew so well.

There were many roes in the meadows grazing, ambling, sometimes fleeing when a stag appeared.

He saw a pheasant stroll along with bobbing head. In three different places he saw festive processions of king pheasants.

"Good," he murmured and let his field glasses drop. "That's good to see. I thank God for this little world unto itself, this forest world of mine, and all its free and lovely creatures."

Again his glance slipped tenderly over treetops which were like great soft green pillows, richly prepared as if for the bed of a giant. His eyes lifted toward the sky arching blue and high over the countryside.

"At this moment, the sky too, is mine," he thought.

For a long time he sat still, his head lifted, his eyes shining. And his heart was full.